W9-BMK-979

Happy Birthday Harlequin
25 Successful Years!
Hope there are many more
Best Wishes
Anne Mather

Dear Reader,

I have a confession to make: I love weddings. Fancy ones, simple ones—it doesn't matter. I end up happily sniffling into a tissue each time. What could be more fun, I thought, than writing about a wedding? Writing about three weddings, that's what! Welcome to the sexy, funny, tender and exciting tales of three brides and three grooms who all meet at—that's right—**a wedding!** Three books, three couples…three terrific stories. Here's the second in the series. You'll enjoy it, even if you haven't read the first, *The Bride Said Never!*—though I hope you have.

Annie Bennett Cooper and her ex-husband, Chase, haven't seen each other since their divorce five years ago. Now their daughter's wedding brings them back together for an afternoon. I can manage it, each one thinks. But neither Annie nor Chase has figured on the things parents will do for the happiness of a child—or on the enduring passion that still sizzles between them in *The Divorcee Said Yes!*

Sit down, relax and enjoy the book. And remember to look for *The Groom Said Maybe!* next month. If you want to drop me a line, I'd love to hear from you. Write to me at P.O. Box 295, Storrs, Connecticut 06268. Please enclose a SASE for a bookmark and a reply.

With my warmest regards,

Sandra Marton

Sandra Marton

SANDRA MARTON

The Divorcee Said Yes!

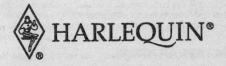

TORONTO • NEW YORK • LONDON
AMSTERDAM • PARIS • SYDNEY • HAMBURG
STOCKHOLM • ATHENS • TOKYO • MILAN • MADRID
PRAGUE • WARSAW • BUDAPEST • AUCKLAND

ISBN 0-373-11962-3

THE DIVORCEE SAID YES!

First North American Publication 1998.

CHAPTER ONE

IT WAS HER DAUGHTER'S wedding day, and Annie Cooper couldn't seem to stop crying.

"I'm just going to check my makeup, darling," she'd told Dawn a few minutes ago, when her eyes had begun to prickle again.

And now here she was, locked inside a stall in the ladies' room of a beautiful old Connecticut church, clutching a handful of soggy tissues and bawling her eyes out.

"Promise me you won't cry, Mom," Dawn had said, only last night.

The two of them had been sitting up over mugs of cinnamon-laced hot chocolate. Neither of them had felt sleepy. Dawn had been too excited; Annie had been unwilling to give up the last hours when her daughter would still be her little girl instead of Nick's wife.

"I promise," Annie had said, swallowing hard, and then she'd burst into tears.

"Oh, Moth-ther," Dawn had said, "for goodness' sake," just as if she were still a teenager and Annie was giving her a hard time about coming in ten minutes after curfew on school nights.

And that was just the trouble. She *was* still a teenager, Annie thought as she wiped her streaming eyes. Her baby was only eighteen years old, far too young to be getting married. Of course, when she'd tried telling that to Dawn the night she'd come home, smiling radiantly with Nick's engagement ring on her finger, her daughter had countered with the ultimate rebuttal.

"And how old were *you* when *you* got married?" she'd said, which had effectively ended the discussion because the whole answer—"Eighteen, the same as you, and look where it got me"—was not one you wanted to make to your own child.

It certainly wasn't Dawn's fault her parents' marriage had ended in divorce.

"She's too young," Annie whispered into her handful of Kleenex, "she's much, much too young."

"Annie?"

Annie heard the door to the ladies' room swing open. A murmur of voices and the soft strains of organ music floated toward her, then faded as the door thumped shut.

"Annie? Are you in here?"

It was Deborah Kent, her best friend.

"No," Annie said miserably, choking back a sob.

"Annie," Deb said gently, "come out of there."

"No."

"Annie." Deb's tone became the sort she probably used with her third-graders. "This is nonsense. You can't hide in there forever."

"Give me one good reason why I can't," Annie said, sniffling.

"Well, you've got seventy-five guests waiting."

"A hundred," Annie sobbed. "Let 'em wait."

"The minister's starting to look impatient."

"Patience is a virtue," Annie said, and dumped the wet tissues into the toilet.

"And I think your aunt Jeanne just propositioned one of the groomsmen."

There was a long silence, and then Annie groaned. "Tell me you're joking."

"All I know is what I saw. She got this look on her face—you know the look."

Annie clamped her eyes shut. "And?"

"And, she went sashaying over to that big blond kid."
Deborah's voice turned dreamy. "Actually I couldn't
much blame her. Did you see the build on that boy?"

"Deb! Honestly!" Annie flushed the tissues down the
toilet, unlocked the stall door and marched to the sink.
"Aunt Jeanne's eighty years old. There's some excuse
for her. But you—"

"Listen, just because I'm forty doesn't mean I'm
dead. *You* may want to pretend you've forgotten what
men are good for, but I certainly haven't."

"Forty-three," Annie said, rummaging in her purse.
"You can't lie about your age to me, Deb, not when we
share a birthday. As for what men are good for—believe
me, I *know* what they're good for. Not much. Not one
damn thing, actually, except for making babies and
that's just the trouble, Dawn is *still* just a baby. She's
too young to be getting married."

"That's the other thing I came in to tell you." Deb
cleared her throat. "He's here."

"Who's here?"

"Your ex."

Annie went still. "No."

"Yes. He came in maybe five minutes ago."

"No, he couldn't have. He's in Georgia or Florida,
someplace like that." Annie looked at her friend in the
mirror. "You're sure it was Chase?"

"Six-two, dirty-blond hair, that gorgeous face with its
slightly off-center nose and muscles up the yin-yang..."
Deb blushed. "Well, I notice these things."

"So I see."

"It's Chase, all right. I don't know why you're so
surprised. He said he'd be here for Dawn's wedding, that
he wouldn't let anyone else give his daughter away."

Annie's mouth twisted. She wrenched on the water,
lathered her hands with soap and scrubbed furiously.

"Chase was always good at promises. It's the follow-through he can't manage." She shut off the faucet and yanked a paper towel from the dispenser. "This whole thing is his fault."

"Annie…"

"Did he tell Dawn she was making a mistake? No. He most certainly did not. The jerk gave her his blessing. His blessing, Deb, can you imagine?" Annie balled up the paper towel and hurled it into the trash can. "I put my foot down, told her to wait, to finish her education. *He* gave her a kiss and told her to do what she thought best. Well, that's typical. Typical! He could never do anything that wasn't just the opposite of what I wanted."

"Annie, calm down."

"I really figured, when he didn't show up for the rehearsal last night, that we'd gotten lucky."

"Dawn wouldn't have thought so," Deb said quietly. "And you know that she never doubted him, for a minute. 'Daddy will be here,' she kept saying."

"All the more proof that she's too young to know what's good for her," Annie muttered. "What about my sister? Has she shown up yet?"

"Not yet, no."

Annie frowned. "I hope Laurel's okay. It's not like her to be late."

"I already phoned the railroad station. The train came in late, or something. It's the minister you've got to worry about. He's got another wedding to perform in a couple of hours, over in Easton."

Annie sighed and smoothed down the skirt of her knee-length, pale green chiffon dress. "I suppose there's no getting out of it. Okay, let's do it… What?"

"You might want to take a look in the mirror first."

Annie frowned, swung toward the sink again and blanched. Her mascara had run and rimmed her green eyes. Her small, slightly upturned nose was bright pink, and her strawberry blond hair, so lovingly arranged in a smooth, sophisticated cap by Pierre himself just this morning, was standing up as if she'd stuck her finger into an electric outlet.

"Deb, look at me!"

"I'm looking," Deb said. "We could always ask the organist if he knows the music from *Bride of Frankenstein.*"

"Will you be serious? I've got a hundred people waiting out there." And Chase, she thought, so quickly and so senselessly that it made her blink.

"What's the matter now?"

"Nothing," Annie said quickly. "I mean...just help me figure out how to repair some of this damage."

Deb opened her purse. "Wash your face," she said, taking out enough cosmetics to start her own shop, "and leave the rest to me."

Chase Cooper stood on the steps of the little New England church, trying to look as if he belonged there.

It wasn't easy. He'd never felt more like an outsider in his life.

He was a city person. He'd spent his life in apartments. When Annie sold the condo after their divorce and told him she was moving to Connecticut, with Dawn, it had damn near killed him.

"Stratham?" he'd said, his voice a strangled roar. "Where the hell is that? I can't even find it on a map."

"Try one of those big atlases you're so fond of," Annie had said coldly, "the ones you look in when you're trying to figure out what part of the country you'll disappear into next."

"I've told you a million times," Chase had snapped, "I have no choice. If I don't do things myself, they get screwed up. A man can't afford that, when he's got a wife and family to support."

"Well, now you don't have to support me at all," Annie had replied, with a toss of her head. "I refused your alimony, remember?"

"Because you were pigheaded, as usual. Dammit, Annie, you can't sell this place. Dawn grew up here."

"I can do what I like," Annie had said. "The condo's mine. It was part of the settlement."

"Because it's our home, dammit!"

"Don't you dare shout at me," Annie had yelled, although he hadn't shouted. Not him. Never him. "And it's not our home, not anymore. It's just a bunch of rooms inside a pile of bricks, and I hate it."

"Hate it?" Chase had repeated. "You hate this house, that I built with my own two hands?"

"You built a twenty-four story building that just happens to contain our particular seven rooms, and you made a million trillion bucks doing it. And, if you must know, yes, I hate it. I despise it, and I can hardly wait to get out of it."

Oh, yeah, Chase thought, shuffling uneasily from one foot to the other and wishing, for the first time in years, that he hadn't given up smoking, oh, yeah, she'd gotten out of the condo, all right. Fast. And then she'd moved herself and Dawn up to this—this pinprick on the map, figuring, no doubt, that it would be the end of his weekly visits with his daughter.

Wrong. He'd driven the hundred-and-fifty-plus miles each way every weekend, like clockwork. He loved his little girl and she loved him, and nothing that had happened between Annie and him could change that. Week after week, he'd come up to Stratham and renewed his bond with his daughter. And week after week, he'd seen that his wife—his former wife—had built herself a happy new life.

She had friends. A small, successful business. And there were men in her life, Dawn said. Well, that was fine. Hell, there were women in his, weren't there? As many as he wanted, all of them knockouts. That was one of the perks of bachelorhood, especially when you were the CEO of a construction company that had moved onto the national scene and prospered.

Eventually, though, he'd stopped going to Stratham. It was simpler that way. Dawn got old enough so she could take a train or a plane to wherever he was. And every time he saw her, she was lovelier. She'd seemed to grow up, right before his eyes.

Chase's mouth thinned. But she hadn't grown up enough to get married. Hell, no. Eighteen? And she was going to be some guy's wife?

It was Annie's fault. If she'd paid a little less attention to her own life and a little more to their daughter's, he wouldn't be standing here in a monkey suit, waiting to give his little girl away to a boy hardly old enough to shave.

Well, that wasn't quite true. Nick was twenty-one. And it wasn't as if he didn't like the kid. Nick—Nicholas, to be precise—was a nice enough young man, from a good family and with a solid future ahead of him. He'd met the boy when he'd flown Dawn and her fiancé to Florida to spend a week with him on his latest job site. The kids had spent the time looking at each other as if the rest of the world didn't exist, and that was just the trouble. It *did* exist, and his daughter hadn't seen enough of it yet to know what she was doing.

Chase had tried to tell her that, but Dawn had been resolute. In the end, he had no choice. Dawn was legally of age. She didn't need his consent. And, as his daughter quickly told him, Annie had already said she thought the marriage was a fine idea.

So he'd swallowed his objections, kissed Dawn, shaken Nick's hand and given them his blessing—as if it were worth a damn.

You could bless the union of two people all you wanted, but it didn't mean a thing. Marriage—especially for the young—was nothing but a legitimate excuse for hormonal insanity.

He could only hope his daughter, and her groom, proved the exception to the rule.

"Sir?"

Chase looked around. A boy who looked barely old enough to shave was standing in the doorway of the church.

"They sent me out to tell you they're about ready to begin, sir."

Sir, Chase thought. He could remember when he'd called older men "sir." It hadn't been so much a mark of respect as it had been a euphemism for "old man." That was how he felt, suddenly. Like an old, old man.

"Sir?"

"I heard you the first time," Chase said irritably and then, because none of what he was feeling was the fault of the pink-cheeked groomsman, he forced a smile to his lips. "Sorry," he said. "I've got the father-of-the-bride jitters, I guess."

Still smiling, or grimacing, whichever the hell it was, he clapped the boy on the back and stepped past him, into the cool darkness of the church.

Annie sniffled her way through the ceremony.

Dawn was beautiful, a fairy-tale princess come to life. Nick was handsome enough to bring tears to whatever eyes weren't already streaming, though not to his former guardian's, who stood beside him wearing a look that spoke volumes on his handsome face.

Chase was wearing the same look. Her ex was not just dry-eyed but stony-faced. He'd smiled only once, at Dawn, as he'd handed her over to her waiting groom.

Then he'd taken his place beside Annie.

"I hope you know what in hell you're doing," he'd muttered, as he'd slipped in next to her.

Annie had felt every muscle in her body clench. How like him, to talk like that here, of all places. And to blame her for—what? The fact that the wedding wasn't being held in a church the size of a cathedral? That there wasn't room for him to invite all his big-shot clients and turn a family event into a networking opportunity?

Maybe he thought Dawn's gown was too old-fashioned, or the flower arrangements—which she, herself, had done—too provincial. It wouldn't have surprised her. As far as Chase was concerned, nothing she'd ever done was right. She could see him out of the corner of her eye, standing beside her, straight and tall and unmistakably masculine.

"Isn't Daddy gorgeous in formal wear?" Dawn had gushed.

A muscle twitched in Annie's cheek. If you liked the type, she supposed he was. But she wasn't a dumb kid anymore, to have her little heart sent into overtime beats by the sight of a man's hard body or equally hard, handsome face.

There had been a time, though. Oh, yes, there'd been a time that just standing next to him this way, feeling his arm brush lightly against her shoulder, smelling the faint scent of his cologne, would have been enough to—would have been enough to—

Bang!

Annie jumped. The doors at the rear of the church had

flown open. A buzz of surprise traveled among the guests. The minister fell silent and peered up the aisle, along with everybody else, including Dawn and Nick.

Somebody was standing in the open doorway. After a moment, a man got up and shut the door, and the figure moved forward.

Annie let out a sigh of relief. "It's Laurel," she whispered, for the benefit of the minister. "My sister. I'm so relieved she finally got here."

"Typical Bennett histrionics," Chase muttered, out of the side of his mouth.

Annie's cheeks colored. "I beg your pardon?"

"You heard me."

"I most certainly did, and—"

"Mother," Dawn snapped.

Annie blushed. "Sorry."

The minister cleared his throat. "And now," he said in tones so rounded Annie could almost see them forming circles in the air, "if there is no one among us who can offer a reason why Nicholas Skouras Babbitt and Dawn Elizabeth Cooper should not be wed..."

A moment later, the ceremony was over.

It was interesting, being the father of the bride at a wedding at which the mother of the bride was no longer your wife.

Dawn had insisted she wanted both her parents seated at the main table with her.

"You can keep your cool, Daddy, can't you?" she'd said. "I mean, you won't mind, sitting beside Mom for a couple of hours, right?"

"Of course not," Chase had said.

And he'd meant it. He was a civilized man and Annie, for all her faults—and there were many—was a civilized woman. They'd been divorced for five years. The wounds had healed. Surely they could manage polite smiles and chitchat for a couple of hours.

That was what he'd thought, but reality was another thing entirely.

He hadn't counted on what it would be like to stand at the altar, with Annie standing beside him looking impossibly young and—what was the point in denying it— impossibly beautiful in a dress of palest green. Her hair had been the wild cluster of silky strawberry curls she'd always hated and he'd always loved, and her nose had been suspiciously pink. She'd sniffled and wept her way through the ceremony. Well, hell, his throat had been pretty tight there, once or twice. In fact, when the minister had gone through all that nonsense about speaking up or forever holding your peace, he'd been tempted to put an arm around her and tell her it was okay, they weren't losing a daughter, they were gaining a son.

Except that it would have been a lie. They *were* losing a daughter, and it was all Annie's fault.

By the time they'd been stuck together at the head of the receiving line as if they were a pair of Siamese twins, he'd felt about as surly as a lion with a thorn in its paw.

"Smile, you two," Dawn had hissed, and they'd obeyed, though Annie's smile had been as phony-looking as his felt.

At least they'd traveled to the Stratham Inn in separate cars—except that once they'd gotten there, they'd had to take seats beside each other at the table on the dais.

Chase felt as if his smile was frozen on his face. It must have looked that way, too, from the way Dawn lifted her eyebrows when she looked at him.

Okay, Cooper, he told himself. Pull it together. You know how to make small talk with strangers. Surely you can manage a conversation with your ex-wife.

He looked at Annie and cleared his throat. "So," he said briskly, "how've you been?"

Annie turned her head and looked at him. "I'm sorry," she said politely, "I didn't quite get that. Were you talking to me?"

Chase's eyes narrowed. Who else would he have been talking to? The waiter, leaning over to pour his champagne?

Keep your cool, he told himself, and bared his teeth in a smile.

"I asked how you've been."

"Very well, thank you. And you?"

Very well, thank you... What was with this prissy tone?

"Oh, I can't complain." He forced another smile, and waited for Annie to pick up the ball. She didn't, so he plunged into the conversational waters again. "Matter of fact, I don't know if Dawn mentioned it, but we just landed a big contract."

"We?" she said, in a tone that could have given chilblains to an Eskimo.

"Well, Cooper Construction. We bid on this job in—"

"How nice," she said, and turned away.

Chase felt his blood pressure shoot off the scale. So much for his attempt at being polite. Annie was not just cutting him dead, she was icing the corpse, craning her neck, looking everywhere but at him.

Suddenly a smile, a real one, curved across her mouth.

"Yoo hoo," she called softly.

Yoo hoo? *Yoo hoo*?

"Hi, there," she mouthed, and waved, and damned if some Bozo the Clown at a nearby table didn't wave back.

"Who is that jerk?" Chase said before he could stop himself.

Annie didn't even look at him. She was too busy looking at the jerk, and smiling.

"That 'jerk,'" she said, "is Milton Hoffman. He's an English professor at the university."

Chase watched as the professor rose to his feet and threaded through the tables toward the dais. The guy was tall, and thin; he was wearing a shiny blue serge suit and he had on a bow tie. He looked more like a cadaver than a professor.

He had a smile on his face, too, as he approached Annie, and it was the smile, more than anything, that suddenly put a red film over Chase's eyes.

"Anne," Hoffman said. "Anne, my dear." Annie held out her hand. Hoffman clasped it in a pasty, marshmallow paw and raised it to his lips. "It was a beautiful ceremony."

"Thank you, Milton."

"The flowers were perfect."

"Thank you, Milton."

"The music, the decorations...all wonderful."

"Thank you, Milton."

"And you look exquisite."

"Thank you, Milton," Chase said.

Annie and the Prof both swung their heads toward him. Chase smiled, showing all his teeth.

"She does, doesn't she?" he said. "Look great, I mean."

Annie looked at him, her eyes flaming a warning, but Chase ignored it. He leaned toward her and hooked an arm around her shoulders.

"Love that low-cut neckline, especially, babe, but then, you know how it is." He shot Hoffman a leering grin. "Some guys are leg men, right, Milty? But me, I was always a—"

"Chase!" Color flew into Annie's face. Hoffman's eyes, dark and liquid behind horn-rimmed glasses, blinked once.

"You must be Anne's husband."

"You're quick, Milty, I've got to give you that."

"He is *not* my husband," Annie said firmly, twisting out of Chase's embrace. "He's my *ex-husband*. My *former* husband. My once-upon-a-time-but-not-anymore husband, and frankly, if I never see him again, it'll be too soon." She gave Hoffman a melting smile. "I hope you've got your dancing shoes on, Milton, because I intend to dance the afternoon away."

Chase smiled. He could almost feel his canine teeth turning into fangs.

"You hear that, Milty?" he said pleasantly. He felt a rush of primal pleasure when he saw Hoffman's face turn even paler than it already was.

"Chase," Annie said, through her teeth, "stop it."

Chase leaned forward over the table. "She's a wonderful dancer, our Annie. But if she's had too much bubbly, you got to watch out. Right, babe?"

Annie opened and shut her mouth as if she were a fish. "Chase," she said, in a strangled whisper.

"What's the matter? Milt's an old pal of yours, right? We wouldn't want to keep any secrets from him, would we, babe?"

"Stop calling me that!"

"Stop calling you what?"

"You know what," Annie said furiously. "And stop lying. I've never been drunk in my life."

Chase's lips curved up in a slow, wicked smile. "Sweetheart, come on. Don't tell me you've forgotten the night we met."

"I'm warning you, Chase!"

"There I was, a college freshman, minding my own business and dancing with my girlfriend at her high school's Valentine Day dance—"

"You were never innocent," Annie snapped.

Chase grinned. "You should know, babe. Anyway, there I was, doing the Mashed Potato, when I spied our Annie, tottering out the door, clutching her middle and looking as if she'd just eaten a bushel of green apples."

Annie swung toward Milton Hoffman. "It wasn't like that at all. My date had spiked my punch. How was I to know—"

A drumroll and a clash of cymbals drowned out her voice.

"...and now," an oily, amplified voice boomed, "Mr. and Mrs. Nicholas Babbitt will take their very first dance as husband and wife."

People began to applaud as Nick took Dawn in his arms. They moved onto the dance floor, gazing soulfully into each other's eyes.

Annie gave Milton a beseeching look.

"Milton," she said, "listen—"

"It's all right," he said quickly. "Today's a family day, Anne. I understand." He started to reach for her hand, caught himself, and drew back. "I'll call you tomorrow. It was...interesting to have met you, Mr. Cooper."

Chase smiled politely. "Call me Chase, please. There's no need to be so formal, considering all we have in common."

Annie didn't know which she wanted to do more, punch Chase for his insufferable behavior or punch Milton Hoffman for being so easily scared off. It took only a second to decide that Chase was the more deserving target. She glared at him as Hoffman scuttled back to his seat.

"You are lower than a snake's belly," she said.

Chase sighed. "Annie, listen—"

"No. No, *you* listen." She pointed a trembling finger at him. "I know what you're trying to do."

Did she? Chase shook his head. Then, she knew more than he did. There wasn't a reason in the world he'd acted like such a jerk just now. So what if Annie was having a thing with some guy? So what if the guy looked as if he might faint at the sight of a mouse? So what if he'd had a sudden, blazing vision of Annie in bed with the son of a bitch?

She could do what she wanted, with whom she wanted. It sure as hell didn't matter to him.

"Are you listening to me?" she said.

Chase looked at Annie. Her face was still shot with color. It arced across her cheekbones and over the bridge of her nose, where a scattering of tiny freckles lay like sprinkles of gold. He remembered how he used to kiss those warm, golden spots after they'd made love.

"I know what you're up to, Chase. You're trying to ruin Dawn's wedding because I didn't do it the way you wanted."

Chase's eyebrows leaped into his hairline. "Are you nuts?"

"Oh, come off it!" Annie's voice quavered with anger. "You wanted a big wedding in a big church, so you could invite all your fancy friends."

"You *are* nuts! I never—"

"Keep your voice down!"

"I am keeping it down. You're the one who's—"

"Let me tell you something, Chase Cooper. This wedding is exactly the kind Dawn wanted."

"And a damn good thing, too. If it had been up to

you, our daughter might have ended up getting married on a hillside in her bare feet—"

"Oh, and what that would have done to Mr. Chase Cooper's image!"

"—while some idiot played a satyr in the background."

"Sitar," Annie hissed. "It's called a sitar, Cooper, although you probably know a lot more about satyrs than you do about musical instruments."

"Are we back to that again?" Chase snarled, and Annie's color heightened.

"No. We are not 'back' to anything. As far as I'm concerned—"

"...the bride's parents, Mr. and Mrs. Chase Cooper."

Annie's and Chase's gazes swung toward the bandstand. The bandleader was smiling benevolently in their direction, and the crowd— even those who looked a bit surprised by the announcement—began to applaud.

"Come on, Annie and Chase." The bandleader's painted-on smile widened. "Let's get up on the dance floor and join the bride and groom."

"Let's not," Chase growled, under his breath.

"The man's out of his mind," Annie snapped.

But the applause had grown, and even the wild glance for help Annie shot toward Dawn, still swaying in the arms of her groom, brought only an apologetic shrug of her daughter's shoulders.

Chase shoved back his chair and held out his hand.

"All right," he said grimly, "let's do it and get it over with."

Annie's chin jerked up. She rose stiffly and put her hand in his.

"I really hate you, Chase."

"The feeling, madam, is entirely mutual."

Eyes hot with anger, Annie and Chase took a couple of deep breaths, pasted civilized smiles on their lips and swung out onto the dance floor.

CHAPTER TWO

IMPOSSIBLE, miserable woman!

That was what she was, his ex-wife, what she'd turned into during the years of their marriage. Chase held Annie stiffly in his arms, enough space between them to have satisfied even starchy Miss Elgar, the chaperone at Annie's Senior Prom.

"Propriety, please," Miss Elgar had barked at any couple daring to get too close during the slow numbers.

Not that she'd approved of the Frug or the Mashed Potato, either. It was just that she'd figured those insane gyrations were safe.

Even all these years later, Chase smiled at the memory. Safe? A bunch of horny kids shaking their hips at each other? And no matter what the old witch thought, the sweetly erotic, locked-in-each-other's-arms slow dancing went on behind her back just the same, in the hallway, in the cafeteria downstairs, even in the parking lot, where the music sighed on the warm spring breeze.

That was where he'd taken Annie, finally, out to the parking lot, where they'd danced, locked in each other's arms, alone in the darkness and so crazy about each other after four months of dating that nothing else had mattered.

That was the night they'd first made love, on an old patchwork blanket he'd taken from the back of his beat-up Chevy and spread on the soft, sweet-smelling grass that grew up on Captree Point.

"We should stop," he'd kept saying, in a voice so thick it had seemed to come from somebody else, though even as he'd said it, he'd been undoing Annie's zipper, removing her gown and baring her beautiful body to his eyes and mouth and touch.

"Yes," Annie had whispered, "oh, yes," but her hands had been moving on him, even as she'd spoken, trembling as she'd undone his silly bow tie, sliding his white dinner jacket from his shoulders, opening his shirt buttons and smoothing her fingers over his hot skin.

The memories surrounded him, as if it were a gentle fog coming in over the sea. Chase made a soft sound in the back of his throat. His arm tightened around his wife; the hand that had been holding hers in stiff formality curled around her wrist, bringing her hand to his chest.

"Chase?" she said.

"Shh," he whispered, his lips against her hair. Annie held herself rigid a second longer, and then she sighed, laid her head against his shoulder and gave herself up to the music and to the memories that had overcome her.

It felt so good to be here, in Chase's arms.

When was the last time they'd danced together this way, not because dancing was what you did at the endless charity functions they'd attended so Chase could "network" with the movers and doers of the business community but simply because there were few things as pleasurable as swaying slowly in each other's arms?

Annie closed her eyes. They'd always danced well together, even back in her high school days at Taft. All those senior parties, the last-minute Friday night get-togethers in somebody's basement rec room the weekends Chase came home from college, and the dance at Chase's fraternity house, when her parents had let her go up for Spring Weekend. The school formals, with Elgar the Dragon Lady marching around, trying to keep everybody at arm's length.

And the night of her senior prom, when they'd finally

gone all the way after so many months of fevered kisses and touches that had left them trembling in each other's arms.

Annie's heartbeat quickened. She remembered Chase taking her out to the parking lot, where they'd moved oh, so slowly to the music drifting from the school gym, and the way Chase had kissed her, filling her with a need so powerful she couldn't think. Wordlessly they'd climbed into his ancient Chevy and made the long drive to the Point, with her sitting so close beside him that they might have been one.

She remembered the softness of the blanket beneath her, after they'd spread it over the grass, and then the wonderful hardness of Chase's body against hers.

"I love you so much," he'd kept saying.

"Yes." She'd sighed. "Yes."

They shouldn't have done it. She'd known that, even as she was opening his shirt and touching him, but to stop would have been to die.

Oh, the feel of him as he'd come down against her naked flesh. The smell of him, the taste of his skin. And oh, that mind-shattering moment when he'd entered her. Filled her. Become a part of her, forever.

Except it hadn't been forever.

Annie stiffened in the circle of her husband's arms.

It had been sex, and eventually, it hadn't been anything at all. He was her ex. That's who Chase was. He wasn't her husband anymore. He wasn't the boy she'd fallen head over heels in love with, nor the man who'd fathered Dawn. He was a stranger, who'd been more interested in his business than in coming home to his wife and child.

More interested in bedding a twenty-two-year-old secretary than the wife whose body had begun to sag and bag.

A coldness seized Annie's heart. Her feet stopped moving. She jerked back and flattened her palms against her former husband's chest.

"That's enough," she said.

Chase blinked his eyes open. His face was flushed; he looked like a man rudely awakened from a dream.

"Annie," he said softly, "Annie, listen—"

"The by-request dancing's over, Chase. The dance floor's filled with people."

He looked around him. She was right. They were on the perimeter of the floor, which was packed with other couples.

"We've played out the necessary charade. Now, if you don't mind, I've reserved the rest of my dance card for Milton Hoffman."

Chase's expression hardened. "Of course," he said politely. "I want to touch bases with some people, too. I see you broke down and invited some of my old friends and not just your own."

"Certainly." Annie's smile would have turned water to ice. "Some of them are my friends, too. Besides, I knew you'd need something to keep you busy, considering that you made the great paternal sacrifice of not asking to bring along your latest little playmate. Or are you between bimbos, at the moment?"

Chase had never struck a woman in his life. Hell, he'd never even had the urge. Men who hit women were despicable. Still, just for an instant, he found himself wishing Annie were a man, so he could wipe that holier-than-thou smirk from her face.

He did the next best thing, instead.

"If you're asking if there's a special woman in my life," he said, his gaze locked on hers, "the answer is yes." He paused for effect, then went for broke. "And

I'll thank you to watch the way you talk about my fiancée.''

It was like watching a building collapse after the demolition guys had placed the dynamite and set it off. Annie's smirk disintegrated and her jaw dropped.

"Your—your…?"

"Fiancée," he said. It wasn't a complete lie. He'd been dating Janet for two months now, and she hadn't been at all subtle about what she wanted from the relationship. "Janet Pendleton. Ross Pendleton's daughter. Do you know her?"

Know her? Janet Pendleton, heiress to the Pendleton fortune? The blond, blue-eyed creature who turned up on the *New York Times* Sunday Society pages almost every week? The girl known as much for the brilliance she showed as vice president at Pendleton as for having turned down a million-dollar offer to lend her classic beauty to a series of perfume ads for a top French company?

For the barest fraction of a second, Annie felt as if the floor was tilting under her feet. Then she drew herself up and pasted a smile on her lips.

"We don't move in the same circles, I'm afraid. But I know who she is, of course. It's nice to see your tastes have gone from twenty-two-year-olds to females tottering on the brink of thirty. Have you told Dawn yet?"

"No! I mean, no, there hasn't been time. I, ah, I thought I'd wait until she and Nick get back from their honey—"

"Milton. There you are." Annie reached out and grabbed Milton Hoffman's arm. She was pretty sure he'd been trying to sneak past her and Chase undetected, en route to the line at the buffet table, but if ever there'd been a time she'd needed someone to cling to, it was now. "Milton," she said, looping her arm through his and giving him a dazzling smile, "my ex has just given me some exciting news."

Hoffman looked at Chase, his eyes wary behind his tortoiseshells. "Really," he said. "How nice."

"Chase is getting married again. To Janet Pendleton." *Could your lips be permanently stretched by a smile*? "Isn't that lovely?"

"Well," Chase said, "actually—"

"I suppose it's the season for romance," Annie said, with a silvery laugh. "Dawn and Nick, Chase and Janet Pendleton..." She tilted her head and gazed up into Milton Hoffman's long, bony face. "And us."

Hoffman's Adam's apple bobbed so hard it almost dislodged his bow tie. It was only a week ago that he'd asked Anne Cooper to marry him. She'd told him how much she liked and admired him, how she enjoyed his company and his attention. She'd told him everything but yes.

His gaze leaped to her former husband. Chase Cooper had taken his father's construction firm and used his engineering degree and his muscles to turn it into a company with a national reputation. He'd ridden jackhammers as they bit deep into concrete foundations and hoisted pickaxes to reduce the remainder to piles of rubble. Hoffman swallowed hard again. Cooper still had the muscles to prove it. Right now, the man looked as if he wanted to use those muscles to pulverize him.

"Chase?" Annie said, beaming. "Aren't you going to wish us well?"

"Yes," Chase said, jamming his hands into his pockets, balling them so hard they began to shake. "I wish you the best, Annie. You and your cadaver, both."

Annie's smile flattened. "You always did know the right thing to say, didn't you, Chase?" Turning on her heel, she propelled herself and Milton off the edge of the dance floor and toward the buffet.

"Anne," Milton whispered, "Anne, my dearest, I had no idea…"

"Neither did I," Annie whispered back, and smiled up into his stunned face hard enough so he'd have to think the tears in her eyes were for happiness and not because a hole seemed suddenly to have opened in her heart.

Married, Chase thought. His Annie, getting married to that jerk.

Surely she had better taste.

He slid his empty glass across the bar to the bartender.

"Women," he said. "Can't live with 'em and can't live without 'em."

The bartender smiled politely. "Yes, sir."

"Give me a refill. Bourbon and—"

"And water, one ice cube. I remember."

Chase looked at the guy. "You trying to tell me I've been here too many times this afternoon?"

The bartender's smile was even more polite. "I might have to, soon, sir. State law, you know."

Chase's mouth thinned. "When I've had too much to drink, I'll be sure and let you know. Meanwhile, make this one a double."

"Chase?"

He swung around. Behind him, people were doing whatever insane line dance was this year's vogue. Others were still eating the classy assortment of foods Annie had ordered and he hadn't been permitted to pay for.

"I've no intention of asking you to foot the bill for anything," she'd told him coldly, when he'd called to tell her to spare no expense on the wedding. "Dawn is

my daughter, my floral design business is thriving and I
need no help from you.''

"Dawn is my daughter, too,'' Chase had snarled, but
before he'd gotten the words out, Annie had hung up.
She'd always been good at getting the last word, dammit. Not today, though. He'd gotten it. And the look on
her face when he'd handed her all that crap about his
engagement to Janet made it even sweeter.

"Chase? You okay?''

Who was he kidding? He hadn't had the last word this
time, either. Annie had. How could she? How *could* she
marry that pantywaist, bow-tie wearing, gender-
confused—

"Chase, what the hell's the matter with you?''

Chase blinked. David Chambers, tall, blue-eyed, still
wearing his dark hair in a long ponytail clasped at his
nape the same way he had since he'd first become
Chase's personal attorney a dozen years ago, was standing alongside him.

Chase let out an uneasy laugh.

"David.'' He stuck out his hand, changed his mind
and clasped the other man's shoulders. "Hey, man,
how're you doing?''

Chambers smiled and drew Chase into a quick bear
hug. Then he drew back and eyed him carefully.

"I'm fine. How about you? You all right?''

Chase reached for his drink and knocked back half of
it in one swallow.

"Never been better. What'll you have?''

Chambers looked at the bartender. "Scotch,'' he said,
"a single malt, if you have it, on the rocks. And a glass
of Chardonnay, please.''

"Don't tell me,'' Chase said with a stilted smile.
"You're here with a lady. I guess the love bug's bitten
you, too.''

"Me?" David laughed. "The wine's for a lady at my table. As for the love bug... It already bit me, remember? One marriage, one divorce...no, Chase, not me. Never again, not in this lifetime."

"Yeah." Chase wrapped his hand around his glass. "What's the point? You marry a woman, she turns into somebody else after a couple of years."

"I agree. Marriage is a female fantasy. Promise a guy anything to nab him, then look blank when he expects you to deliver." The bartender set the Scotch in front of David, who lifted the glass to his lips and took a swallow. "The way I see it, a man's got a housekeeper, a cook and a good secretary, what more does he need?"

"Nothing," Chase said glumly, "not one thing."

The bartender put a glass of Chardonnay before David, who picked it up. He turned and looked across the room. Chase followed his gaze to a table where a cool-looking, beautiful brunette sat in regal solitude.

A muscle knotted in David's jaw. He took another swallow of Scotch.

"Unfortunately," he said, "there is one other thing. And it's what most often gets poor bastards like you and me in trouble."

Chase thought of the feel of Annie in his arms on the dance floor, just a couple of hours ago.

"Poor bastards, is right," he said, and lifted his glass to David. "Well, you and I both know better. Bed 'em and forget 'em, I say."

David laughed and clinked his glass against Chase's. "I'll drink to that."

"To what? What are you guys up to, hidden away over here?"

Both men turned around. Dawn, radiant in white lace and with Nick at her side, beamed at them.

"Daddy," she said, kissing her father's cheek. "And Mr. Chambers. I'm so glad you could make it."

"I am, too." David held his hand out to her groom. "You're a lucky man, son. Take good care of her."

Nick nodded as the men shook hands. "I intend to, sir."

Dawn kissed Chase again. "Get out and circulate, Daddy. That's an order."

Chase tossed her a mock salute. The bridal pair moved off, and he sighed. "That's the only good thing comes of a marriage. A kid, to call your own."

David nodded. "I agree. I'd always hoped..." He shrugged, then picked up his drink and the glass of white wine. "Hey, Cooper," he said, with a quick grin, "you stand around a bar long enough, you get maudlin. Anybody ever tell you that?"

"Yes," Chase said. "My attorney, five years ago when we got wasted after my divorce was finalized."

The men smiled at each other, and then David Chambers slapped Chase lightly on the back.

"Take Dawn's advice. Circulate. There's a surprising assortment of good-looking single women here, in case you hadn't noticed."

"For a lawyer," Chase said with a chuckle, "sometimes you manage to come up with some pretty decent suggestions. What's with the brunette at your table? She spoken for?"

David's eyes narrowed just the slightest bit. "She is, for the present."

"Yeah?"

"Yeah," the attorney said. He was smiling, but there was a look in his eye that Chase recognized. He grinned.

"You dirty dog, you. Well, never mind. I'll—what did my daughter call it? Circulate. That's it. I'll circulate, and see what's available."

The men made their goodbyes. Chase finished his drink, refused to give the bartender the satisfaction of telling him he wouldn't pour him another, and circulated himself right out the door.

Annie kicked off her shoes, put her feet up on the old chintz-covered ottoman she kept promising herself she'd throw out and puffed out a long, deep sigh.

"Well," she said, "that's over."

Deb, seated opposite her on the sofa, nodded in agreement.

"Over and done with." She flung her arms along the top of the sofa and kicked off her shoes, too. "And I'll bet you're glad it is."

"Glad?" Annie pursed her lips and blew a very unladylike raspberry. "That doesn't even come close. I'll bet Custer had an easier time planning the battle at Little Bighorn than I had, planning this wedding."

Deb arched a dark, perfect eyebrow. "Bad analogy, if you don't mind my saying so."

"Yeah." Annie heaved another sigh. "But you know what I mean. The logistics of the whole thing were beyond belief. Imagine your daughter walking in one night and calmly announcing she's going to get married in two months and wouldn't it be wonderful if she could have the perfect wedding she'd always dreamed about?"

Deb stood, reached up under her chiffon skirt and wriggled her panty hose down her legs.

"My daughter's in love with the seventies," she said, draping the hose around her throat like a boa. "If I'm lucky, she'll opt for getting married on a hilltop somewhere, with the guests all invited to bring… What's the matter?"

"Nothing." Annie shot to her feet and padded to the kitchen, returning a moment later with a bottle of champagne and a pair of juice glasses. "He accused me of wanting that, you know."

"Know what? Wanting what? Who accused you?"

"You mind drinking this stuff out of juice glasses? I know you're supposed to use flutes, but I never got around to buying any."

"We can drink it out of jelly jars, for all I care. What are you talking about, Annie? Who accused you of what?"

"Chase. Mr. Ex." Annie undid the wire around the foil, then chewed on her lip as she carefully worked the cork between her fingers. It popped with a loud bang and champagne frothed out. Some of it dripped onto the tile floor. Annie shrugged and mopped it up by moving her stockinged foot over the small puddle. "A few weeks ago, he called to talk to Dawn. I had the misfortune to answer the phone. He said he'd gotten his invitation and he was delighted to see I hadn't let my instincts run amok." She held out a glass of wine, and Deb took it. "Amok," she said, licking her fingertips, "can you imagine? And all because when we were first married, I threw a couple of parties in the backyard behind the house we lived in."

"I thought you lived in a condo."

"We did, eventually, but not then. Chase knew somebody who got us this really cheap rental in Queens."

Deb nodded. "What kind of parties did you throw?"

"Outdoor parties, mostly."

"So?" Deb made a face. "Big deal."

Annie's lips twitched. "Well, it was wintertime."

"Wintertime?"

"Yes. See, the thing was, the house was so small, the mice pretty much ran it. And—"

"Mice?"

Annie sank down on the chair again. "It wasn't much

of a house, but then, we didn't have much money. I'd just graduated from high school and the only job I could find was at the local Burger King. Chase had transferred to City College. The tuition was lots cheaper and besides, that way he could work construction jobs for his father a couple of days a week.'' She sighed. ''We were dead broke. Believe me, we found a million ways to save money!''

Deb smiled. ''Including having parties outdoors in midwinter.''

Annie smiled, too. ''Oh, it wasn't that bad. We'd build a fire in a barbecue in the backyard, you know? And I'd make tons and tons of chili and homemade bread. We'd put on a huge pot of coffee, and there'd be beer for the guys...''

Her voice drifted away.

''A far cry from today,'' Deb said. She reached for the champagne bottle and refilled both their glasses. ''Bubbly, caviar, shrimp on ice, boneless beef with mushrooms...''

''*Filet de Boeuf Aux Chanterelles*, if you please,'' Annie said archly.

Deb grinned. ''*Pardonnez-moi, madam.*''

''No joke. Considering what that stuff cost, you'd better remember to give it its French name.''

''And you didn't let Chase pay a dime, huh?''

''No,'' Annie said sharply.

''I still think you're nuts. What're you trying to prove, anyway?''

''That I don't need his money.''

''Or him?'' Deb said softly. Annie looked at her and Deb shrugged. ''I saw you guys on the dance floor. Things looked pretty cozy, for a while there.''

''You saw the past worm its way into the present.

Trust me, Deb. That part of my life is over. I don't feel a thing for Chase. I can't quite believe I ever did.''

"I understand. A nostalgia trip, hmm?''

"Exactly. Brought on by my little girl's wedding…'' Annie paused, swallowed hard and suddenly burst into tears.

"Oh, sweetie.'' Deb jumped from the couch and squatted down beside Annie. She wrapped her arms around her and patted her back. "Honey, don't cry. It's not so unusual to still have a thing going for your ex, you know. Especially when he's hunky, the way Chase is.''

"He's getting married,'' Annie sobbed.

"Chase?''

"To Janet Pendleton.''

"Am I supposed to know her?''

"I hope not.'' Annie hiccuped. "She's rich. Gorgeous. Smart.''

"I hate her already.'' Deb put her hand under Annie's chin and urged it to rise. "Are you sure?''

"He told me so.'' Annie sat back, dug a hanky out of her cleavage where she'd stuffed it after the ceremony and blew her nose. "So I told him I'm marrying Milton.''

"Milton? As in, Milton Hoffman?'' Deb rocked back on her heels. "My God, you wouldn't!''

"Why not? He's single, he's dependable and he's nice.''

"So is a teddy bear,'' Deb said in horror. "Better you should take one of those to bed than Milton Hoffman.''

"Oh, Deb, that's not fair.'' Annie got to her feet. "There's more to a relationship than sex.''

"Name it.''

"Companionship, for one thing. Similar interests. Shared dreams.''

"And you can have enough of those things with Milton to make you forget all the rest?"

"Yes!" Annie's shoulders slumped. "No," she admitted. "Isn't that awful? I like Milton, but I don't love him."

Deb heaved a sigh as she stood up. "Thank you, God. For a minute there, I thought you'd gone around the bend."

"Not only am I sex-obsessed—"

"You're not. Sex is a big part of life."

"—but I've used poor Milton badly. Now I've got to call him up and tell him I didn't mean it when I introduced him to Chase as my fiancé."

"Wow," Deb said softly. "You certainly have had a busy day."

"A messy day, is what you mean."

"Don't kill me for saying this, but maybe you should rethink things. I mean, I know he's getting married and all, but maybe you do still have a thing for your ex."

"I wouldn't care if he were living in a monastery!" Annie's eyes flashed. "I do not have a 'thing' for Chase. I admit, I'm upset, but it's because my baby's gotten herself married."

"You know what they say, Annie. We only raise children to let go of them once they grow up."

Annie tucked the hanky back into her cleavage, picked up the champagne bottle and headed for the kitchen.

"It's not letting go of her that upsets me, Deb. It's that she's so young. Too young, I'm afraid, to make such a commitment."

"Well," Deb said, folding her arms and leaning against the door frame, "you were young when you got hitched, too."

Annie sighed. "Exactly. And look where it led me. I thought I knew what I was doing but it turned out I didn't. It was hormones, not intelligence, that—'' The phone rang. She reached out and picked it up. "Hello?"

"Annie?"

"Chase." Annie's mouth narrowed. "What do you want? I thought we said all we needed to say to each other this afternoon."

Across town, in his hotel room, Chase looked at the boy standing at the window. The boy's shoulders were slumped and his head was bowed in classic despair.

Chase cleared his throat.

"Annie... Nick is here."

Annie's brows knotted together. "Nick? There? Where do you mean, there?"

"I mean he's here, in my room at the Hilton."

"No. That's impossible. Nick is on a plane to Hawaii, with Dawn..." The blood drained from Annie's face. "Oh God," she whispered. "Has there been an accident? Is Dawn—"

"No," Chase said quickly. "Dawn's fine. Nothing's happened to her, or to Nick."

"Then why—"

"She left him."

Annie sank down into a chair at the kitchen table. "She left him?" she repeated stupidly. Deb stared at her in disbelief. "Dawn left Nick?"

"Yeah." Chase rubbed the back of his neck, where the muscles felt as if somebody were tightening them on a rack. "They, uh, they got to the airport and checked in their luggage. Then they went to the VIP lounge. I upgraded their tickets, Annie, and bought them a membership in the lounge. I knew you wouldn't approve, but—"

"Dammit, Chase, tell me what happened!"

Chase sighed. "Nick said he'd get them some coffee.

Dawn said that was fine. But when he came back with the coffee, she was gone.''

"She didn't leave him," Annie said, her hand at her heart, "she's been kidnapped!"

"Kidnapped?" Deb snapped. "Dawn?"

"Did you call the police? Did you—"

"She left a note," Chase said wearily. Annie heard the rustle of paper. "She says it's not that she doesn't care for him."

"Care for him?" Annie's voice rose. "People *care* for—for flowers. Or parakeets. She said she loved Nick. That she was crazy about him."

"…not that she doesn't care for him," Chase continued, "but that loving him isn't enough."

"Isn't—?"

"Isn't enough. She says she has no choice but to end this marriage before it begins."

Annie put her hand over her eyes. "Oh God," she whispered. "That sounds so ominous."

Chase nodded, as if Annie could see him.

"Nick's beside himself, and so am I." His voice roughened with emotion. "He's looked for her everywhere, but he can't find her. Dear God, If anything's happened to our little girl…"

Annie's head lifted. As soft as a whisper, the front door opened, then closed. Footsteps came slowly down the hall.

"Mom?"

Dawn stood in the doorway, dressed in the going-away suit they'd bought together, the corsage of baby orchids Annie had pinned on the jacket's lapel sadly drooping. Dawn's eyes were red and swollen.

"Baby?" Annie whispered.

Dawn gave Annie a smile that trembled, and then a sob burst from her throat.

"Oh, Mommy," she wailed, and Annie dropped the phone and opened her arms. Her daughter flew across the room and buried her face in her mother's lap.

Deb picked the phone up from the floor.

"Chase?"

"Dammit to hell," Chase roared, "who is this? What's going on there?"

"I'm a friend of Annie's," Deb said. "You and Nick can stop worrying. Dawn's here. She just came in."

Chase flashed an okay sign to Nick, who hurried to his side.

"Is my daughter okay?"

"Yes. She seems to—"

Chase slammed down the phone, and he and Nick ran out the door.

CHAPTER THREE

THE MOON HAD RISEN, climbed into a bank of clouds, and disappeared.

Sighing, Chase switched on the lamp beside his chair and wished he could pull a stunt like that. Maybe then people would stop looking at him as if he might just come up with a solution to an impossible situation.

But the simple truth was that impossible situations required improbable solutions, and he didn't have any. His mind was a blank. At this point, he wasn't even sure what day it was. The only thing he knew for certain was that a few hours ago, he'd been the father of—the bride. Now he was the father of—what did you call a young woman who'd gotten to the airport and then told her brand-new husband that they'd made an awful mistake and she wanted out?

Smart. That was what Chase would have called her, twenty-four hours ago, when he'd have given just about anything if Dawn had decided to put her wedding off until she was older and, hopefully, wiser.

Chase closed his eyes wearily. But his daughter *hadn't* decided to put off her wedding. She'd gone through with it, which put a different spin on things. More than canceling arrangements with the church and the caterer were involved here. Dawn and Nick were bound together, in the eyes of God and in accordance with the laws of the state of Connecticut.

Severing that bond was a lot more complicated than it would have been a few hours ago. And it sure didn't help that Dawn kept weeping and saying she loved Nick with all her heart, it was just that she couldn't, wouldn't, mustn't stay married to him.

Chase put his hand to the back of his neck and tried to rub the tension out of his muscles. He had no idea what she was talking about, and neither did Nick, the poor, bewildered bastard. Not even Annie understood; Chase was certain of that, and never mind the way she'd kept saying, "I understand, sweetheart," while she'd rocked Dawn in her arms.

"*What* do you understand?" Chase had asked her in exasperation, when she'd come hurrying out of the bedroom after she'd finally convinced Dawn to lie down and try to get some sleep. Annie had shot him one of those men-are-so-stupid looks women did so well and said she didn't understand *anything*, but she wasn't about to upset Dawn by telling her that.

"Dammit, Annie," Chase had roared, and that had done it. Nick had come running, Dawn had started crying, Annie had called him a name he hadn't even figured she knew…hell, he thought wearily, it was a good thing Annie didn't have a dog, or it would have gotten in on the act and taken a chunk out of his ankle.

"Now see what you've done," Annie had snarled, and the door to Dawn's room had slammed in his bewildered face.

Chase groaned. He was tired. So tired. There'd been no sound from behind the closed door for hours now. Annie and his daughter were probably asleep. Even Nick had finally fallen into exhausted slumber on the sofa in the living room.

Maybe, if he just put his head back for a five-minute snooze…

"Dammit!"

Chase's head bobbed like a yo-yo on a string. That was just what he'd needed, all right. Oh, yeah. Nothing like a little whiplash for neck muscles that already felt knotted.

"Stupid chair," he muttered, and sprang to his feet.

For a minute there, he'd forgotten he wasn't in the den he and Annie had shared for so many years. Annie had dumped all the old furniture when she'd bought this house. She'd filled these rooms with little bits and pieces of junk. Antiques, she called them, but junk is what the stuff was. Delicate junk, at that. Sofas and tables with silly legs, chairs with no headrests...

"You kick that chair, Chase Cooper, and I swear, I'll kick you!"

Chase swung around. His ex-wife stood in the entrance to the room. She'd exchanged her mother-of-the-bride dress for a pair of jeans and a sweatshirt and from the way her hair was standing on end and her hands were propped on her hips, he had the feeling her mood wasn't much better than his.

Too bad. Too damned bad, considering that she was the one had gotten them into this mess in the first place. If only she hadn't been so damned permissive. If only she'd put her foot down right at the start, told Dawn she was too young to get married—

"It deserves kicking," he grumbled, but he stepped aside and let her swish past him, snatch up the chair cushions and plump them, as if that might remove any sign he'd sat there. "How's Dawn?"

"She's asleep." Annie tucked the cushions back in place. "How's Nick? I assume he's still here?"

"Yes, he's here. He's asleep, in the living room."

"And he's okay?"

"As okay as he can be, all things considered. Has our daughter told you yet just what, exactly, is going on?"

Annie looked at him. Then she ran her fingers through her hair, smoothing the curls back from her face.

"How about some tea?" Without waiting for his answer, she set off for the kitchen. "Unless you'd prefer coffee," she asked, switching on the overhead fluorescent light.

"Tea's fine," Chase said, blinking in the sudden glare. He sank onto one of the stools that stood before the kitchen counter, watching as Annie filled a kettle with water and put it on the stove. "Has she?"

"Has she what?" Annie yanked open the pantry door. She took out a box of tea bags and put it on the counter. "Would you like a cookie? Of course, I don't have those hideous things you always preferred, with all that goo in the middle."

"Just tea," he replied, refusing to rise to the bait. "What did Dawn say?"

Annie shut the pantry door and opened the refrigerator. "How about a sandwich? Swiss? Or there's some ham, if you prefer."

"Annie…"

"You'd have to take it on whole grain bread, though, the kind you always said—"

"—that I wouldn't touch until somebody strapped a feed bag over my face and a saddle on my back. No, thank you very much, I don't want a sandwich. I don't want anything, except to know what our daughter told you and what it is you don't want to tell me." Chase's eyes narrowed. "Has Nick mistreated her?"

"No, of course not." Annie shut the refrigerator door. The kettle had begun to hiss, and she grabbed for it before it could whistle. "Hand me a couple of mugs, would you? They're in that cupboard, right beside you."

"He doesn't seem the type who would." Chase grabbed two white china mugs and slid them down the counter to Annie. "But if he's so much as hurt a hair on our daughter's head, so help me—"

"Will you please calm down? I'm telling you, it isn't that. Nick's a sweetheart."

"Well, what is it, then?"

Annie looked at him, then away. "It's, ah, it's complicated."

"Complicated?" Chase's eyes narrowed again. "It's not—the boy isn't..."

"Isn't what? Do you still take two sugars, or have you finally learned to lay off the stuff?"

"Two sugars, and stop nagging."

Annie dumped two spoonfuls of sugar into her ex's tea, and stirred briskly.

"You're right. You can wallow in sugar, for all I care. Your health isn't my problem anymore, it's hers."

"Hers?"

"Janet Pendleton."

"Janet Pen..." He flushed. "Oh. Her."

Annie slapped the mug of tea in front of him, hard enough so some of the hot amber liquid sloshed over the rim and onto his fingers.

"That's right. Let your fiancée worry about your weight."

"Nobody's got to worry about my weight," Chase said, surreptitiously sucking in his gut.

He was right, Annie thought sourly, as she slid onto the stool next to his. Nobody did. He was still as solid-looking and handsome as he'd been the day they'd married—or the day they'd divorced. Another benefit of being male. Men didn't have to see the awful changes that came along, as you stood at top of the yawning chasm that was middle age. The numbers that began to creep upward on your bathroom scale. The flesh that began to creep downward. The wrinkles that Janet Pendleton didn't have. The sags Chase's cute little secretary hadn't had, either.

"…make him normal. That's not what happened with Dawn and Nick, is it?"

Annie frowned. "What are you talking about?"

"Reality, that's what. I was telling you that I just heard about this guy, married a girl even though he knew he was a switch hitter, hoping that having a wife would make him normal—"

Annie choked over her tea. "Good grief," she said, when she could speak, "you are such a pathetic male stereotype, Chase Cooper! No, Nicholas is not, as you so delicately put it, a 'switch hitter.'"

"You're sure?"

"Yes."

"Yeah, well, it might not hurt to ask."

"Nick and Dawn have been living together, the past three months. And Dawn hasn't so much as hinted at any problem in bed. Quite the contrary." Annie blushed. "I dropped in a couple of times—not in the morning, or late at night, you understand—and I could pretty much tell, from the time it took them to get to the door and the way they looked, that things were perfectly fine in that department." She looked down at her tea. "I don't drop by without calling first, anymore."

"What do you mean, they've been living together?"

"Just what I said. Didn't Dawn tell you? They took an apartment, in Cannondale."

"Dammit, Annie, how could you permit our daughter to do that?"

"To do what? Move in with the man she was going to marry?"

"Didn't you tell her no?"

"She's eighteen, Chase. Legally of age. Old enough to make her own choices."

"So?"

"What do you mean, 'so'?"

"You could have told her it was wrong."

"Love is never wrong."

"Love," Chase said, and shook his head. "Sex, is more like it."

"I asked her to take her time and think it through, to be sure she was doing the right thing. She said she'd done that, and that she was."

"Sex," Chase said again.

Annie sighed. "Sex, love…they go together."

"Yeah, well, they could have had the one and still waited for the other, until after the wedding." Chase glowered into his tea. "But I suppose that's too old-fashioned."

"It was, for us."

Chase looked up sharply. Color swept into his face. "What we did, or didn't do, has nothing to do with this situation."

"That's where you're wrong." Annie stood. She picked up her mug of tea, cupped it with both hands and walked to the deep bow window that overlooked the garden. "I'm afraid we have everything to do with this situation."

"What are you talking about?"

"Do me a favor, will you? Shut off the light. My head's pounding like a drum."

"You want some aspirin?"

Annie shook her head. "I already took some." She sat down on the sill, her knees drawn up to her chin, her eyes on the darkness beyond the glass. "You want to know what Dawn said? Okay, I'll tell you, but you're not going to like it."

"I don't like much of anything that's already happened today," Chase said, getting to his feet and walking toward her. "Why should this be any different?"

"The first thing she said was that she loves Nick."

"Uh-huh." Chase folded his arms and leaned back against the window frame. "Why do I get the feeling we're about to play, 'good news, bad news'?"

"She said she knows that he loves her."

"That's the good news, right?"

Annie nodded. "The bad news is that she ran away from him for the same reason."

Chase's brows knotted. "Let me be sure I'm following this. Our daughter fell in love, got engaged, moved in with the guy, married him, went off with him on her honeymoon...and then decided to bolt because it dawned on her that she loves him and he loves her?"

Annie sighed. "Well, it's a bit more complicated than that."

"I'm relieved to hear it. For a second there, I thought I was going completely nuts. What's the rest?"

"She's afraid."

"She's afraid," Chase said, trying to stay calm. He had the feeling they were moving into the sort of emotional deep water that women swam through effortlessly and men found way over their heads. "Of what?"

"Of them falling out of love."

"Annie." Chase sat down on the sill, his knee brushing hers. "You just said, girl loves boy. Boy loves girl. They're just starting out. There's no reason for her to think—"

"She's afraid of what's going to happen."

Chase waited, but Annie said nothing. He could almost see the water rising.

"What's going to happen?" he said carefully.

Annie shrugged. "Their love will shrivel up and die."

"That's ridiculous."

"I said the same thing."

"And?"

"And, she said..." Annie swallowed hard. "She said she'd watched us today, at the wedding."

"Us?" Chase nodded, as if he had a clue as to what they were talking about. The only thing he was sure of was that the water was definitely getting deeper. And rougher. "As in you, and me?"

"Us," Annie repeated, "as in you, and me. She said it hurt her to see how we hated being forced into each other's arms, on the dance floor."

"Well, of course we did. Nobody warned us that was going to happen. Did you explain that to her?"

"I did."

Chase thought back to the moment when Annie had gone into his arms. He thought beyond that, to when he'd suddenly realized how good it had felt to have her there, and he cleared his throat.

"We managed, didn't we?"

"Sure. I pointed that out to her."

"And?"

"And, she said it was sad, that—that we'd had to pretend we enjoyed dancing together again." Annie's cheeks grew warm. She could clearly recall the instant when being held in Chase's arms had gone from being an unwanted chore to being—to being... She took a deep breath. "I told her it was nothing for her to worry about."

"And?"

"And, that was it."

"What was it? I don't know what the hell you're talking about."

Annie put her mug on the sill beside her. Then she linked her hands together in her lap.

"That was what triggered it."

"Triggered what? I still don't know what—"

"Dawn said she was standing at the airport ticket

counter, just standing there, you know, while Nick checked their luggage through and confirmed their seats, and all of a sudden it struck her that what was really so sad about you and me was that once upon a time, we must have loved each other a great deal.''

''She'd have liked it better if we hadn't?''

Annie swallowed. Her throat felt uncomfortably tight. ''She said—she said that she realized, for the first time, that you and I must have felt just the way she and Nick feel. You know, as if we were the only two people on the whole planet who'd ever loved each other so much.''

''Lovers always feel that way,'' Chase said gruffly.

''She said that if her mother and father could go from feeling like that to—to feeling the way we do about each other now, then she didn't want any part of the process that got them—that got us—to this point.''

Chase stared at his ex-wife. Her eyes were glassy with unshed tears and her mouth was trembling. Was she remembering, as he was, how it had once been between them? The joy? The passion? After a long minute, he cleared his throat again.

''What'd you say?''

''What could I say?''

''That our mistakes don't have to be hers, for starters.''

Annie waved her hand in a sad little gesture of dismissal.

''Did you tell her that she was probably tired and jittery, and overdramatizing things?''

''Yes.''

''Good.''

''I thought so, too.'' Annie sighed. ''But Dawn said she was just being pragmatic. She said she'd rather end things between her and Nick now, while they still cared for each other, than wait until—until they hated each other.''

"God, Annie. We don't hate each other. You told her that, didn't you?''

Annie nodded.

"And?''

"And she said I was kidding myself, that love and hate were two sides of the same coin, that there was no middle ground, once people who'd been in love fell out of love.''

Chase blew out his breath. "My daughter, the philosopher.''

Annie looked up, her eyes filling again. "What are we going to do?'' she whispered.

"I don't know.''

"Dawn's heart is breaking. There's got to be something! We can't just let her walk away from Nick. She loves him, Chase. And he loves her.''

"I know. I know.'' Chase shoved his hand through his hair. "Let me think for a minute.''

"Our daughter's terrified of marriage, and it's our fault!''

Chase shot to his feet. "That's crap.''

"It's the truth.''

"It isn't. It's bad enough we couldn't make *our* marriage work but I'll be damned if I'm going to feel guilty for the failure of Dawn's marriage. You hear me, Annie?''

"The entire house will hear you,'' Annie hissed. "Keep your voice down, before you wake the kids.''

"They're not 'kids.' Didn't you just tell me that? Our daughter was old enough to decide she was ready to get married even though, according to you, you tried to talk her out of it.''

"According to me?'' Annie leaped up, her hands on

her hips. "I *did* try to talk her out of it! But you'd already caved in and given her the 'follow your heart' baloney. You told her to do what she wanted!"

"That's not true." Chase strode toward Annie, his eyes blazing. "I begged her to think and think again. I said she was too damned young to take such a serious step—and guess what? I was right."

Annie's shoulders slumped. "Okay, okay. So we both tried to convince her to wait. So maybe she should have listened to us. But she didn't."

"No. She didn't. She did her own thing. And then she sees us dancing and all of a sudden, she turns into Sigmund Freud and figures out that she's made a terrible mistake."

"Chase, please! Keep your voice—"

"She has an epiphany, brought on by seeing us dancing. Why not by a gum wrapper on the floor at the airport, or the electrical energy from an overhead wire?"

"This is not something to joke about, dammit!"

"Maybe it was some guy at a piano, playing a three-handed version of 'The Man That Got Away.'" Chase lifted his arms to the sky, then dropped them to his sides. "What was wrong with her hearing the day her old man tried to give her some advice?"

"It was advice I'd tried to give her, too," Annie said coldly. "I keep telling you that."

"What was the use of my talking," Chase said, ignoring her, "if she wasn't listening? She did what she wanted and now she thinks she can lay it off on our divorce?" Chase's mouth thinned. "I don't think so."

"She's not trying to lay anything off. She's upset."

"*She's* upset? What about everybody else? Does she think we're busy yakking it up and having an all-around good time?" Chase's face darkened. "Do you know what it was like, having Nick turn up at the door to tell me Dawn had run off and he couldn't find her? Do you have any idea at all of what that kid and I went through?''

"Yelling won't help, Chase."

"Neither will playing the patsy." Chase rammed his fist against the wall. "If only you'd put your foot down sooner."

"Dammit," Annie said fiercely, "I did!"

"I don't know what you did. I wasn't here for the past five years, remember?"

"And whose fault was that?"

Chase and Annie glared at each other, and then Annie blew out her breath.

"This is pointless. There's no sense bringing up the past. Dawn needs our help. We can't let her walk away from Nick and her marriage for the wrong reasons."

"I agree. Damn, if only she'd made do with simply moving in with Nick. Why'd she have to rush into marriage?"

"A little while ago, you were furious because she *had* moved in with him!"

"Didn't you teach her any self-control? If she hadn't let her hormones get the best of her—"

"How dare you? How *dare* you talk about self-control? If you'd had any self-control at all, we might still be married!"

"I'm tired of defending myself against that old charge, Annie. Besides, if you hadn't treated me as if I had leprosy—"

"That's right. Blame it on me."

"I don't see anybody else in this room to blame it on."

"I hate you, Chase Cooper! I hate you, do you hear? And I regret every time I ever let you touch me!"

"Liar!"

"Liar, am I?"

Chase reached out, caught Annie's shoulders and yanked her to him. "You were like warm butter, in my arms, right from the beginning."

"Only because I was so innocent!" Annie set her teeth and tried to twist free. "I was a baby when we met. Or have you forgotten that?"

"You were the hottest baby I'd ever seen. The first time I kissed you, you were like fireworks going up. All I could think of was having you to myself, for the rest of my life."

"Except when you found out there was more to life than bed."

"Oh, yeah," he said, his lips pulling back from his teeth, "yeah, you sure taught me that lesson. 'Not now, Chase. I'm not in the mood, Chase.'"

"And whose fault was that, do you think?"

"You didn't see me rolling over and turning my back to you, did you, babe?"

"Don't 'babe' me," Annie said furiously. "And if I rolled away from you, it was for a darn good reason. I didn't feel anything anymore. Did you expect me to pretend?"

"Is that what you do when you're with Hoffman? Do you pretend he turns you on?"

Annie's hand shot through the air, but Chase caught her wrist before she could connect with his jaw.

"You know damn well you didn't have to pretend when I made love to you," he growled, "even at the end. You were just too proud to admit it."

"Poor Chase. Can't your ego take the truth?"

"I'll show you 'truth'!"

"No," Annie said, but it was too late, Chase had already pulled her into his arms, and brought his mouth to hers.

His kiss was filled with anger and Annie struggled

against it, pounding her fists against his shoulders, trying desperately to tear her mouth from his.

And then, deep within her, something seemed to let go.

Maybe it was the stillness of the night, curling just outside the window. Maybe it was the unyielding tension of the endless day. Suddenly anger gave way to a far more dangerous emotion. Hunger. The hunger that had been between them in the past and that she'd believed dead.

Chase felt it, too.

"Annie," he whispered, against her mouth. His hands swept into her hair, lifting her face to his. With a sigh of surrender, her arms went around his neck, her lips parted beneath his, and she gave herself up to him and to the kiss.

It was like a dance once learned and never forgotten. Their bodies shifted, moving against each other with an ease that came of passion long-ago shared. Their heads tilted, their lips met, their tongues sought and tasted. Annie clasped her hands behind Chase's neck; he slid his slowly down her body, cupped her bottom and lifted her into him. She whimpered when she felt the hardness of him against her; he groaned when he felt her tilt her hips to his.

For long moments, they were lost to everything but each other. Then, breathing hard, they stepped apart.

Annie's skin felt hot when Chase cupped her face in his hands and brushed a light kiss on her lips. He wanted to lift her into his arms and carry her into the darkness.

"Annie?" he whispered, and she smiled and clasped his wrists with her hands.

"Yes." She sighed...

Suddenly the kitchen blazed with light.

"Mom? Dad? What on earth are you doing?"

Annie and Chase spun around. Dawn and Nick stood in the doorway, openmouthed with shock.

CHAPTER FOUR

IT WAS, Annie thought, the question of the decade.

What *were* they doing, she and her former husband?

Her cheeks, already scarlet, grew even hotter.

Making out as if they were a pair of oversexed kids, that was what. She and Chase had been wrapped around each other as if it were years and years ago, when he'd just brought her home from a date. In those days, not even an hour spent parked on that little knoll half an hour's drive north of the city, steaming up the windows of Chase's old Chevy, had been enough to keep them from wanting just one more kiss, one more caress.

"Mother?"

Dawn was still staring at them both. She looked as if finding her parents kissing was only slightly less shocking than it would be if she'd found the kitchen populated with little green men saying, "Take me to your leader."

And, Annie thought grimly, it was all Chase's fault.

He'd taken advantage of her distress, capitalized on her already-confused emotions. And for what possible reason?

To shut her up.

It was the same old ploy he'd used during the years that their marriage had been falling apart. She'd try to talk about what was wrong and Chase, who was perfectly happy with their marriage as it was, would say there was nothing to discuss. And if she persisted, he'd shut her up by taking her in his arms and starting to make love.

It had worked, but only for a very little while, when

she'd still been foolish enough to think those kisses meant he loved her. Eventually she'd figured out that they meant nothing of the sort. Chase was just silencing her, in the most direct way possible, using what had always worked best between them.

Sex. Raw, basic, you-Jane, me-Tarzan sex.

But sex, no matter how electric, just wasn't enough when the rest of the relationship had gone wrong. It had taken her a while to realize that, but realize it she had.

He was playing the same ugly game tonight. And she'd made it easy. Responding to him, when she knew better. Kissing him back, when she didn't feel anything for him. Whatever had seemed to happen, in his arms just now, was a lie. She *didn't* feel anything for Chase, except anger.

"Mother? Are you all right?"

Annie took a deep, deep breath.

"Fine," she said, and cleared her throat. "I'm perfectly fine, Dawn."

A puzzled smile broke across Dawn's mouth. She looked from Annie to Chase.

"What were you guys doing?"

Annie waited for Chase to respond, but he remained silent. That's right, she thought furiously. Let me be the one to figure out something to say. He knew, the rat, that she wouldn't tell Dawn the truth, wouldn't say, "Well, Dawn, your no-account old man was on the losing end of an argument so he did what he always used to do whenever that happened..."

"Well," Annie said, "well, your father and I were, ah, we were talking about you. And Nick. And—and—"

"And your mother began to cry, so I put my arms around her to comfort her."

Annie swung toward Chase. He was standing straight and tall, the portrait of honor, decency and paternalism in his chinos, open-collared shirt and long-sleeved, forest-green cashmere sweater. His hair was a little ruffled and he had end-of-day stubble on his jaw, but on him—she hated to admit—it looked good.

She, on the other hand, was a mess. Old jeans. Old sweatshirt. Hair that had been allowed to dry without benefit of a dryer or a brush, and a face that was painfully free of even the most basic makeup.

"Your poor mother is very upset," Chase said, putting his arm around Annie's shoulders and giving her his best "chin-up" smile. "She needed a shoulder to cry on. Isn't that right, Annie?"

"Right," Annie said, through a smile that was all clenched teeth. What else could she do? Blurt out that Chase was lying? That the two of them had been standing in the dark, locked in a kiss that had left her knees buckling, because he was a manipulative bastard and she was too long without a man? That was the truth, wasn't it? The real truth. She'd never have responded to him if she hadn't been living like a nun.

"Really?" Dawn looked at them both again, and then the faint smile that had been lifting her lips trembled and fell. "I understand. It was foolish of me to think... I mean, when I saw you guys kissing, I thought... I almost thought... Oh, never mind."

"Kissing?" Annie said, with a slightly wild laugh. She stepped carefully out of Chase's encircling arm, went to the stove and began making what had to be the hundredth pot of tea she'd made this evening. "Kissing, your father and me?"

"Uh-huh." Dawn slouched to the table, pulled out a chair and dropped into it. She propped her elbows on the table and rested her chin in her cupped hands. "Kissing. Just goes to show how utterly dumb I can be."

"No," Nick said quickly. Everyone looked at him. It

was the first word to come out of his mouth since he and Dawn had switched on the light. His fuzz-free cheeks pinkened under the scrutiny of his bride and her parents. "You aren't."

"I am. Getting married when anybody with half a brain could see it was a mistake, because marriage doesn't last. We all know that."

"We don't know any such thing," Nick said, hurrying to her. He squatted beside her chair and reached for her hands, taking them gently in his.

"Just look around you, Nicky. Your guardian, your uncle Damian? Divorced. My parents? Divorced. Even Reverend Craighill—"

"The guy who performed the ceremony?" Chase said. Dawn nodded.

"How do you know that?"

"I asked him. The poor man's been divorced twice. Twice, can you imagine?"

Chase shot a look at Annie. "No," he said tightly, "I certainly can't."

"Don't look at me that way," Annie snapped. The teakettle let out a piercing whistle and she snatched it from the stove. "What has the man's marital history to do with anything?"

"A minister who can't keep his wedding ring on ought to consider going into some other kind of work," Chase growled.

"No," Dawn said, "he's in the right kind of work, Daddy. He's a reminder of reality." She sighed again. "I just wish I'd been smart enough to realize all this before today instead of being so darned dumb."

"Sweetheart, stop saying that." Nick clasped her shoulders. "You were smart to fall in love with me, smarter still to marry me." He shot an accusatory look at Chase and Annie. "As for thinking you saw your folks kissing when we turned on the light—you were right.''

Dawn's head came up. ''I was?''

''Absolutely. I saw them, too.''

''No,'' Annie said.

''We weren't,'' Chase added.

''Not at all,'' Annie argued, waving her hand in her ex's direction. ''Dawn, your father already explained what happened. I was upset. He was trying to comfort me.''

''You see, Nicky?'' Dawn's eyes filled with tears. ''They weren't kissing. Oh, how I wish they had been.''

Annie frowned. ''You do?''

''Of course.'' Dawn snuffled and wiped the back of her hand across her nose. Annie and Chase both reached for the paper towels, but Nick pulled a handkerchief from his pocket and handed it to his wife, who blew into it. ''See, when I saw you in Daddy's arms, well, when I thought I saw you in his arms, it was such a big thing that I felt happy for the first time since Nick and I got to the airport. I figured, just for a second, I admit, but still, I figured…''

''You figured what?'' Annie said, softly, even though she already knew, even though it broke her heart to think that her daughter still harbored such useless dreams, such futile hopes. She went to Dawn's side, looped her arm around her shoulders and kissed the top of her head. ''What, darling?''

Dawn took a shuddering breath. ''I figured that a miracle had occurred today,'' she whispered, ''that you and Daddy had finally realized what a mistake you'd made in splitting up and that you still loved each other.''

There was a pained silence. Then a soft sob burst from Annie's throat.

''Oh, Dawn. Darling, if it were only that simple!''

"You can't judge the future of your marriage by the failure of ours," Chase said gruffly. "Sweetie, if you and Nick love each other—"

"What does that prove? You and Mom loved each other, once."

"Well, sure. Of course we did, but—"

"And then you fell out of love, like everybody else."

"Not everybody, sweetie. That's an awfully broad state—"

"It must have been awful, knowing you'd loved each other and then having things fall apart."

Chase looked at Annie. Help me with this, his eyes flashed, but she knew she had no more answers now than she'd had five years ago.

"Well," he said carefully, "yes, yes, it wasn't pleasant. But that doesn't mean—"

"You guys did your best to keep me out of it, but I wasn't a baby. I used to hear Mom crying. And I saw how red your eyes were sometimes, Daddy."

Nick got to his feet and stepped back as Chase reached for his daughter's hand.

"We never meant to hurt you, Dawn. We'd have done anything to keep from hurting you."

"You don't understand, Daddy. I'm not crying over the past, I'm crying over the future. Over what's almost definitely, positively, absolutely going to happen to Nicky and me. I don't know why it took me so long to realize. We'll—we'll break each other's hearts, is what we'll do, and I'd rather walk away now than let that happen."

Annie smoothed her daughter's hair from her forehead. "Dawn, honey, I can point to lots of marriages that have succeeded."

"More fail than succeed."

"I don't know where you got that idea."

"It's not an idea, it's a fact. That Family Life course I'm taking at Easton, remember? My instructor showed us all these statistics, Mom. Marriage is a crapshoot."

Annie gritted her teeth, silently calling herself a fool for having convinced Dawn that she ought to at least attend classes at the local community college, now that she wasn't going to go away to school as they'd planned.

"There's an element of risk in anything that's really worthwhile," Chase said.

Annie gave him a grateful look. "Exactly."

"So, when people get married, they should be aware that they're taking a gamble?" Dawn said, looking from her mother to her father.

Annie opened her mouth, then shut it. "Well, no. Not exactly," she said, and cleared her throat. "People shouldn't think that." She looked at Chase again. *Say something*, was written all over her face.

"Of course not," Chase said quickly. "A man and a woman should put all their faith in their ability to make their marriage succeed."

"And if that turns out not to be enough?"

"Then they should try harder."

Dawn nodded. "And then they should give up."

"No! What I mean is…" It was Chase's turn to look at Annie for support. "Annie? Can you, ah, explain this?"

"What your father is saying," Annie said, stepping gingerly onto the quicksand, "is that sometimes a man and a woman try and try, and they still can't make a relationship work."

"Like you and Daddy."

Annie could feel the sand shifting, ever so slowly, under her feet.

"Well, yes," she said slowly, "like us. But that doesn't mean all marriages are failures."

Dawn sighed. "I guess. But other people's marriages don't mean much to me right now. All I could think of today was how wonderful it would be if you guys got back together again." She buried her nose in Nick's handkerchief and gave a long, honking blow. "And then, when I saw you guys kissing…when I *thought* I saw you kissing…"

"We were," Chase said. Annie's head sprang up as if somebody had jabbed her with a pin. He saw the look of disbelief she flashed him but hell, there was no reason to lie about something as simple as a kiss. He laced his fingers through Dawn's and smiled gently at her. "You didn't imagine that, sweetheart. You and Nick were right. I was kissing your mother. And she was kissing me back."

Dawn's tearstained face lit.

"You mean…" She looked at them, her lips trembling. "I was right? You guys are thinking of getting together again?"

"No," Annie said quickly. "Dawn, a kiss doesn't mean—"

"It doesn't mean they've reached any decisions," Nick said. "Right, Mrs. Cooper?"

Oh, Nick, Annie thought unhappily. She rose to her feet and put her hand on his arm. "Look, I know what you both would like to hear me say, but—"

"Just say there's a chance," Nick said, his eyes pleading with hers for time, for hope, for understanding. "Even a little one."

Annie could feel the delicate pull of the quicksand at her toes. "Chase," she said urgently, "please, say something!"

Chase swallowed hard. It was years since Annie had looked at him this way, as if he were her knight in shining armor. Dawn, too. He couldn't remember his daughter turning to him since she'd stopped skinning her knees playing softball.

Both his women needed him to come to their rescue.

It was a terrific feeling. Unfortunately he hadn't the faintest idea how to do it.

Think, he told himself, dammit, man, think! There had to be something...

Dawn's eyes filled again. "Never mind. You don't have to spell it out for me. I'm old enough to understand that a kiss isn't a commitment."

Annie let out a breath that felt as if she'd been holding forever.

"That's right," she said.

"It was stupid of me to think that you guys were going to give it another try."

Annie smiled at Chase over their daughter's head.

"I'm glad you understand that, sweetie."

"There are no second chances, not in this life." Dawn wiped her nose and looked at the trio gathered around her. "That's from Kierkegaard. Or maybe Sartre. One of those guys, I forget which."

"Your philosophy course," Annie said grimly, mentally ripping in half the tuition check she'd just mailed to Easton Community College.

"Of course there are," Chase said sharply.

"No," Dawn said, sighing, "there aren't. Just look at you two, if you want a perfect example."

"All right," Chase said, "I've had enough."

"Chase," Annie said, "don't say anything you'll regret."

"Mr. Cooper, sir, as Dawn's husband—"

"Dawn Elizabeth Cooper... Dawn Elizabeth *Babbitt*, you're behaving like a spoiled child." Chase nudged Nick aside, put his hands on his hips and glared down at his daughter. "This is all nonsense. Marriage statistics, divorce statistics, and now quotes from a bunch of dead old men who wouldn't have been able to find their—"

"Chase," Annie said sharply.

"—their hats on their heads, when they were still alive and kicking." Chase squatted down in front of Dawn. "You and Nick love each other. That's the reason you got married. Right?"

"Right," Dawn said, in a small voice. "But, Daddy—"

"No, you listen to me, for a change. I gave you your turn, now you give me mine." Chase took a deep breath. "You loved each other. You got married. You took some very important vows, among them the promise to stay together through the bad times as well as the good. Think about that promise, Dawn." He took her hands in his and looked into her teary eyes. "It means, you've always got to give it a second chance. It means, love doesn't die, it only gets lost sometimes, and if you loved each other once, there's always damn good reason to think you can find it again."

Dawn nodded, the tears streaming down her face.

"Exactly," she said. "That's why, when I saw you and Mom together I thought, isn't it wonderful? They've decided to give themselves another chance."

"Dawn," Nick said, "please, darling. You're upset."

"I am not," Dawn said in a shaky whisper.

"Let's get out of here. Let's give *us* a chance."

"What for? So we can break our hearts someplace down the road?" A sob caught in her throat. "You're asking me to take a terrible gamble, Nick, and to do that would take a miracle."

"Yes!" The word seemed to leap, unbidden, from Chase's throat. Every head in the room snapped in his direction.

"Yes?" Annie said. "Yes, what?"

Chase stared at his former wife's pale face. It was a terrific question. What had he said yes to? Despite all his arguments, he knew his daughter was right. A frighteningly high percentage of marriages failed. And the breakup, when you'd loved someone as deeply as he'd once loved Annie, was the worst pain imaginable.

But how could he let his daughter and her groom fail before they'd even tried? Nick had the right idea. He and Dawn had to get away from here. They had to be alone and unpressured. They had to go on their honeymoon, and Chase could think of only one way to make that happen.

His daughter wanted a miracle? Okay. He'd give her one.

"Yes, you were right, about your mother and me."

"No," Annie said. "Chase, don't!"

"We didn't want to say anything until we were certain, because it isn't certain yet, you understand, it's far from certain, in fact, it's very, very uncertain and altogether iffy—"

"Chase!" Annie cried, her voice high and panicked, but hell, he'd gone too far to stop now.

So he ignored Annie, gave Dawn his most ingratiating smile and shot a quick prayer in the direction of the ceiling, just in case anybody who kept track of white lies was listening.

"No promises," he said, "and absolutely no guarantees because, frankly, I don't think the odds are too good but yeah, your mother and I have decided to at least talk about giving things between us a second chance."

CHAPTER FIVE

CHASE WATCHED as Annie paced the length of the living room.

It was almost hypnotic. She went back and forth, back and forth, pausing before him each time just long enough to give him a look that had gone from anger to disbelief to a glare that would have brought joy to the heart of the Medusa.

Aside from a quick burst of fury after Dawn and Nick had left, she had yet to say anything to him, but that was hardly reassuring. Another explosion was just a matter of time. Her white face, thinned mouth and determined pacing told him so. And he could hardly blame her.

What in heaven's name had impelled him to do such a stupid thing? To even suggest there was a possibility of reconciliation had been crazy. It was wrong. Hell, it was unfair. Dawn, falsely convinced she'd had her miracle, had gone off with hope in her heart...

But at least she'd gone. That was what he'd wanted, after all, to give his daughter time to be alone with her husband, time to realize that the future of her marriage was not linked to the failure of his and Annie's.

Just because one generation screwed things up didn't mean the next one would, too.

Chase felt the weight lifting from his shoulders. What he'd done had been impetuous, perhaps even outrageous. But if it gave Dawn time to find her own way through the minefield of life and marriage, it was worth it. Who had he hurt, really? When the kids got back from their honeymoon—happy, he was certain, and concentrating on their future instead of his and Annie's—he'd explain that he'd misled them, just a little bit.

"And just how do you think she's going to feel, when you tell her you lied?"

Chase looked up. Annie had come to a stop in front of him. Her sweatshirt inexplicably but appropriately featured a picture of Sesame Street's Oscar the Grouch. Her face was white, her eyes shiny and she was so angry she was trembling.

Angry—and incredibly beautiful.

A lifetime ago, she used to tremble that way when she lay in his arms. When he touched her. When he stroked her breasts, and her belly. When he moved between her silken thighs...

"Do you hear me, Chase Cooper? How do you think our daughter will feel, when she finds out her miracle is a bucket of hogwash?"

Chase frowned. "It isn't as bad as that."

"You're right. It's worse."

"Look, I was just trying to help her."

"Hah!"

"Okay, okay. Maybe I made a mistake, but—"

"Maybe?" Her voice shot up the scale, her eyebrows to her hairline. "*Maybe* you made a mistake?"

"The words just came out. I didn't mean—"

"Can't you even admit you were wrong?"

"I already did. I said maybe I made a mistake."

Annie snorted. "You still don't see it, do you! A 'mistake' is when a person forgets an appointment. Or dials a wrong number."

"Or says something, in the heat of the moment, that he thinks might—"

"You lied, Chase. There's a big difference. But I'm not surprised."

Chase rose to his feet. "And what, exactly, is that supposed to mean?"

"Nothing," Annie said coldly, and turned away.

"Dammit!" He grabbed her shoulder and swung her around to face him. "If there's one thing I never could stand, it was that word. 'Nothing,' you always say, but even an idiot can tell you really mean 'something.'"

Annie smiled sweetly. "I'm happy to hear it."

Dark color swept into his face. He clutched her tighter and leaned toward her.

"You're pushing your luck, babe."

"Why?" Her chin lifted. "What are you going to do, huh? Slug me?"

Annie saw Chase's eyes narrow. What had made her say such a thing? They had quarreled, yes. Fought furiously with words. By the time they'd agreed to divorce, they'd hurled every possible bit of invective at each other.

But he'd never hit her. He'd never raised his hand to her. She'd never been afraid of him physically and she wasn't now.

It was just that she was so angry. So enraged. He was, too. And just a little while ago, when he'd been mad and she'd been mad, he'd ended up hauling her into his arms and kissing her until her toes had tingled.

For Pete's sake, woman, are you insane? Are you trying to tick him off so he'll kiss you again?

She stiffened, then twisted out of his grasp.

"This isn't getting us anywhere," she said. She walked to the sofa and sat down. "I just wish I knew what to do next."

"Why should we have to 'do' anything?" Chase said, sitting down in the chair.

"Dawn's going to have such expectations..."

Chase sighed and leaned forward, his elbows on his knees. He put his head in his hands.

"Yeah."

"How could you? How *could* you tell her that?"

"I don't know." He straightened up and passed his hand over his face. "Exhaustion, maybe. I haven't slept in—what year is this, anyway?"

"To tell her such nonsense—"

"Yeah, yeah," he said, "okay, you made your point." He frowned and shifted his backside on the cushion of the contraption Annie called a chair, where he'd spent the last hour being tortured. "What's this damn chair stuffed with, anyway? Steel filings?"

"Horsehair, which should be just right, considering that you are, without question, the biggest horse's patootie I ever did know!"

Chase gave a bark of incredulous laughter. "Patootie? Goodness gracious, land's sakes alive, Miss Annie, what out and out vulgarity!"

"Dammit, Chase—"

"Oh my. Better watch yourself, babe. Your language is slipping."

"Don't 'babe' me. I don't like it. Just tell me what we're supposed to do now."

Chase winced as he got to his feet. He rubbed the small of his back, then massaged his neck, and walked slowly to the window.

The sun was a slash of lemon yellow as it rose in the deep woods behind the house. Dawn was almost here— and *his* Dawn was almost there, in Hawaii, beginning her honeymoon with Nick. He smiled and thought of sharing the play-on-words with Annie, but he suspected she might not see the humor in the situation.

"We wait until the kids come home," he said, turning around and looking at Annie, "and then we tell—*I* tell them—that I should never have claimed we were going to give things another try.''

''The truth, you mean.''

''The whole truth, and nothing but the truth. Yes.''

Annie nodded. She stood up and walked toward the kitchen. Chase followed her.

''I suppose that will clear your conscience.''

Chase eased onto a stool at the counter.

''Look, I know it won't be that easy, but—''

He winced as Annie slammed a cupboard door shut.

''Unfortunately,'' she said, ''it won't do a thing for mine.''

''If you're going to make another pot of coffee or tea—''

''That's exactly what I'm going to do.''

''Not for me.'' He put a hand against his flat belly. ''The last dozen cups are still gurgling around in my stomach.''

''Maybe you'd rather have something else. Hot chocolate?''

Chase's brows lifted. ''Well, yeah, that might be—''

''Hemlock, perhaps. A nice, big cup.''

''There's no need to behave like that, Annie.''

''No?''

''No.'' He stood up, went to the refrigerator and opened it. ''Isn't there any beer?''

''There is not.'' Annie slid under his arm and slammed the fridge door shut. ''I,'' she said self-righteously, ''do not drink beer.''

Chase looked at her. ''I'll just bet the poetry pansy doesn't drink it, either.''

''The…?'' Annie flushed. ''If you mean Milton—''

''How about some diet Coke? Or is that beneath you, too?''

Annie shot him an angry glare. Then she stalked to the pantry door and pulled it open.

"Here," she said, jamming the can of soda at him. "Have a Coke, even though it's only six in the morning. Maybe it'll clear your head enough so you can come up with a plan that'll work."

"I already did." Chase yanked the pull tab on the can and made a face as he downed a mouthful of warm soda. "I told you," he said, as he took a tray of ice cubes from the freezer, dumped some into a glass and added the Coke. "When the kids come back from their honeymoon, I'll tell them that we stretched the truth a little for their own good."

"We?" Annie said, in an ominously soft voice.

"Okay. Me. I did it. I stretched the truth."

"You're stretching it now, Chase. Say it. You lied."

Chase took a long drink, then put the cold glass against his forehead.

"I lied. All right? Does that make you feel better?"

"Yes." Annie frowned. "No." She looked at him for a long minute. Then she turned and stared at the coffee, dripping slowly from the filter basket into the carafe. "You lied, and what did I do?"

"Look, I don't know what you're trying to accomplish here, Annie, but we just went around with this, remember? I was the black-hearted horse's whatever-you-called-me that started us on this path into the pits of hell." He sighed, then laid the hand clutching the glass of Coke over his heart. "You want me to swear I'll come clean? I will. You want my word I'll make it crystal clear you didn't do anything? I'll do that, too."

Annie folded her arms over her chest. "But I did."

"Did what? God, I have been up for more hours than there are in a day, and my brain is starting to whimper.

What's wrong now? I said I'd tell Dawn it was all my idea. I can't do any more than that, babe, can I?''

Annie plunked herself onto a stool. "Don't call me that," she said, but without her usual fire. She sighed deeply. "You can't tell her I'm not part of it because the truth is that I was."

"Was what?" Chase said, trying to keep his patience. He looked at his half-filled glass of soda, and wondered if there was more caffeine in it or in a cup of coffee. "I'm tired," he muttered. "I need to lie down, Annie. I'm worse than tired. I could have sworn I heard you say—"

"I did." Annie put her elbows on the counter and scrubbed her face with her hands. "I said, I'm as responsible for this mess as you are."

"Don't be ridiculous. I was the one who lied."

"At least you're admitting that it *was* a lie." She sighed, scrubbed her face again and then looked up at him and folded her hands neatly on the countertop. "Dawn's going to ask me why, if I knew you were lying, I didn't say anything."

"Well, you'll tell her the truth."

"Which is?"

"Which is..." Chase frowned. "I don't know what we're talking about anymore! The truth is the truth."

"The truth isn't the truth. Not exactly. I mean, I heard you tell her that we're thinking about a reconciliation. I could have said 'That isn't so, Dawn. Your father's making it up.'"

Chase felt a tightening in his chest.

"But you didn't," he said.

"I didn't." Annie looked at him, then at her hands, still folded before her. "I kept quiet."

"Why?" Her hair had fallen forward, curling around

her face. He fought the urge to reach out and touch the soft, shining locks.

Annie sighed. "You'll call me crazy."

"Try me."

"Because, in my heart, I knew it was the only way to get her to stop comparing herself and Nick to us. It was a foolish thing for her to be doing. Just because you and I—because we fell out of love, doesn't mean they will, too." She looked up, her expression one of defiance. "Well?"

Something indefinable swept through him. Relief, he told himself. Hell, what else could it be?

"I won't call you crazy." He smiled. "But you've got to admit, you're up to your backside in the murky waters of what's a lie and what's a fib, the same as me."

Annie nodded. "Well then, when they get back, we both admit that we fudged the truth and hope for the best."

"I suppose."

Annie's mouth trembled. "Dawn's going to be hurt. And angry."

"She'll get over it."

"We never lied to her about anything, Chase. Even when—when we finally decided to end our marriage, we told her the truth."

Chase looked at his ex-wife.

"Well," he said carefully, "perhaps there's another way." He watched as Annie wiped her hands over her eyes. "I mean..." He forced his lips into a tight smile. "I mean, we could agree to go ahead with a reconciliation."

"What?"

"Not a real one, of course," he said quickly. "A pretend one. You know, spend some time together. Go out for dinner, talk. That kind of thing."

Annie stared at him. Her eyes were wide and very dark. "Pretend?"

"Well, sure." Chase spoke briskly, almost gruffly. "Just so we could look the kids straight in the eye and say yeah, we tried…"

"No."

"No?"

Annie shook her head. "I—I couldn't."

"Why not?"

Annie struggled to find an answer. Why not, indeed? What would it take, for her to spend the week of Dawn's honeymoon dating—pretending to date—her former husband? They could avoid pushing the buttons that stirred up old animosities and pain. They could shake hands, as if this were a business deal, and pretend, for their daughter's happiness.

But she couldn't do it. A week, seeing Chase? Seven days, smiling at him over dinner? Seeing his face, hearing his voice? Walking at his side? No. It would be too—too—

"It would be wrong," she said brusquely.

"Annie…"

"There's no reason to compound one lie with another." She rose, picked up the coffeepot and dumped the contents into the sink. "You were right. One more mouthful of caffeine and I'm going to start twitching."

"Annie…"

"What?" She swung around and faced him. "It wouldn't work," she said flatly. "Not for you, not for me—not for anybody else."

"Who else? Nobody'd need to know."

Annie drew herself up. "What about your fiancée?"

"My…?"

"Janet Pendleton. How would you explain it to her?"

Chase frowned. Another lie, coming back to bite him

in the tail. "Well," he said, "well, I'd just tell her—I'd say…" His eyes focused on Annie's. "I'll tell her whatever it is you'd tell your pansy poet."

Annie flushed. "That's one thing about you, Chase Cooper. You always did have a way with words. I thought I told you, Milton is a professor at the college."

"He's a limp-wristed twit, and I'll bet anything you're taking one of his dumb courses. What is it this time? How To Speak Sixteenth-Century English In A Twenty-First Century World? Fifty Ways To Turn Simple Thoughts Into Total Obfuscation?"

"Obfuscation," Annie said, batting her lashes. "I'm impressed."

"Yeah, well, I'm not. How can you be so gullible? Flocking to dumb courses given by jerks with too many initials after their names…"

"You have a lot of initials after your name, Mr. Cooper. But, of course, you're not a jerk."

"You're damn right, I'm not. At least I've got some calluses on my hands. I know the meaning of honest labor."

"Sorry, Chase. You've lost the right to use that word. 'Honest' does not apply, after the whopper you told our daughter."

"Is that how you met him?"

"Who?"

"Hoffman. Am I right? Did you take a course he taught?"

"Milton is a Shakespearean scholar with an outstanding reputation."

"In what? Seducing married women?"

Annie's eyes flashed. "I am not a married woman. Yes, I took a course he taught and yes, he writes poetry. Beautiful poetry, which I'm sure is beyond your comprehension. Unfortunately, since I know it'll disappoint you to hear this, Milton is not gay.''

Chase folded his arms over his chest. "I suppose you speak from personal experience," he said, and felt his stomach clench.

Annie barely hesitated. Why worry about telling a lie to the master of the art? "Of course," she said, with a little smile.

Chase's jaw tightened. This was a moment for some cleverly sarcastic remark. Unfortunately, his mind was a blank. No, that wasn't true. It had filled with an image of Annie in Hoffman's arms, of his fist connecting with Hoffman's narrow jaw.

"How nice for you both," he said coldly.

Annie tossed her head. "We think so."

"So, when's the big day?"

"What big…?" She swallowed. "You mean, the wedding?" She shrugged and mentally crossed her fingers. "We, ah, we haven't set an actual date yet. And you?"

"And me, what?"

"When are you and Janet tying the knot?"

Knot was right. Chase could feel the noose, slipping around his throat.

"Soon."

"This summer?"

"It depends. I've got this project starting in Seattle."

"And, of course, that comes first."

"It's an important job, Annie."

"I'm sure it is. And I'm sure Janet understands that."

"She does, yes. She knows it takes twenty hours out of a twenty-four-hour day to take a firm like the one my old man left me to the top."

"Better her than me."

"You're damned right!"

They glared at each other, both of them remembering—just in case it had slipped their minds—how glad they were not to be living with each other anymore, and then Chase turned away.

"I've got a plane to catch," he said.

"That's it. Just take off. Turn your back on the mess you made."

"Dammit, what would you like me to do? I'm due in Seattle for a site inspection tomorrow afternoon. Hell, what am I talking about?" Frowning, he pushed back the sleeve of his sweater and checked his watch. "It's *this* afternoon."

"Run away," Annie said coldly, folding her arms, "before we've even finished talking or found a solution to the problem *you* created."

"Fine. You want to talk? You can drive me to my hotel so I can pick up my things. Then you can drive me to the airport."

Fifteen minutes to his hotel, Annie thought, eyeing him narrowly, and then forty more to Bradley Airport. One hour, more or less. Surely she could survive that much time in his company if it meant they might come up with a plan.

"All right," she said, then hesitated. Maybe she should go upstairs and change...? No. What for? Chase deserved to be driven to the airport by a woman in an Oscar the Grouch sweatshirt.

"Well?" she said impatiently, sweeping her car keys from a hook on the wall. "What are you waiting for, Chase? Let's go."

Annie waited in her car while Chase collected his suitcase from his hotel room.

Offering to drive him to the airport hadn't been such a great idea.

They hadn't come up with one single good idea during the time it had taken them to get here. And sitting so close to Chase in the bucket seats of her little Honda made her, well, uncomfortable. He was too big for the car. His thigh was right there, an inch from her own. His shoulder brushed hers, on a tight turn, and his after-shave wafted in the air.

The sooner she got rid of him, the better.

"Okay," she said, once he was seated beside her again, "what airline?"

"West Coast. Something like that." He dug into his pocket as she pulled the car into traffic. "Here's the ticket. West Coast Air, that's it."

"How original," Annie said with a tight smile. "Must be new. What terminal is it at? A or B?"

"What do you mean, A or B?"

"Bradley's got two terminals," she said patiently. "One's A. One's B. I need to know which we're going to."

"We're not going to Bradley."

Annie looked at him. "We're not?"

"I'm flying out of Logan. In Boston. I thought you understood that."

Boston. A two-hour drive, instead of forty minutes. Annie's hands felt sweaty on the steering wheel.

"Boston," she said faintly. "I don't think…"

"My flight leaves at noon. Will we make it? Maybe I should phone the airline. If there's another flight in an hour or two, we could stop for a bite to eat first."

"Don't be silly." Annie glanced at the dashboard clock. "I'll get you there in plenty of time," she said, and jammed her foot to the floor.

They got to the airport with twenty minutes to spare.

Annie stopped her car at a stretch of curb marked No

Parking. Chase opened his door and got out.

"Well," he said, "thanks for the lift."

She nodded. "You're welcome."

"Sorry we didn't come up with a solution."

"Yes. Me, too."

"As soon as the kids get home…"

"I'll call you."

"We'll figure out something, by then."

"Sure."

"Dawn's a good kid. She'll understand, if we decide to make a clean breast of things."

"Chase. Your plane."

"Oh. Right. Right." Chase slammed the car door. "Well…"

"Goodbye," Annie said. She stepped on the gas and drove off.

A block away, she pulled to the curb. Her heart was racing and her eyes felt grainy.

Why had they quarreled over so many silly things? Why had they sniped at each other?

"Because you're mismatched," she whispered, answering her own questions. "You were always mismatched. It's just the sex that kept you from realizing the truth—"

Annie frowned. What was that, on the floor in front of the passenger seat? She bent down and scooped a long white envelope from the floor.

It was Chase's airline ticket.

"Damn," she said, and threw the car into a rubber-burning U-turn.

He wasn't in the terminal, or maybe he was. There were people milling around everywhere; how could she be certain?

Annie raced to look at the Departures screen. Where had he said he was going? Seattle, that was it. On West Coast Air. There it was. Gate Six.

She flew through the ticket area, through the lounge, toward the gate. She almost stopped at the security checkpoint when the guard asked to see her ticket, but then she remembered that was the reason she was here, that she *had* a ticket clutched in her hand, and she waved it at him and hurried through.

Where was Chase?

There! There he was! Her relief at finding him diminished everything else, including how he'd managed to clear security without a ticket.

"Chase," she yelled, "Chase!"

He turned at the sound of her voice. "Annie?" She saw his face light. "Annie," he said again, and opened his arms.

She told herself later that she hadn't meant to run to him, that she'd simply been going too fast to stop. But the next thing Annie knew, she was locked in Chase's embrace.

"Annie," he said softly, "baby."

And then her arms were around his neck and his hands were in her hair and they were kissing.

"Chase," she whispered shakily, "your ticket…"

"It's okay," he said, against her lips. "Don't talk. Just kiss me."

She did, and it was just the way it had always been. The sweetness of the kiss. The sheer joy of it, and then the rush of excitement that came of being in Chase's arms…

"Mom! Dad! Isn't this incredible?"

Annie and Chase sprang apart. Dawn and Nick were standing perhaps three feet away. Nick looked a little surprised, but Dawn's face showed only absolute delight.

Annie recovered first.

"Dawn?" she said. "And Nick. What are you doing here?"

"Yes." Chase cleared his throat. "We thought you'd, ah, we thought you'd flown out hours ago."

"Well, there was a delay. Weather. Something like that. Nothing serious."

"Great," Chase said heartily. "I mean, that's too bad. I mean... Listen, I wish I could stay and talk to you guys, but my plane—"

"We were just walking around to kill time. Are you on this flight to Seattle?"

"Yes. And it's going to be leaving in a couple of minutes, so—"

"Sure." Dawn came forward and gave them each a hug. "I think it's wonderful," she said, smiling at her parents. "You two, doing this."

"Dawn," Annie said, "baby..."

"Annie," Chase said carefully.

She looked at him. He was right. This was hardly the time to tell their daughter about their subterfuge.

"What, Mom?"

"Just—just keep an open mind, okay? About—about your father and me."

Dawn nodded and settled into the curve of her husband's arm.

"I will."

"Good. That's good. Because—"

"I just want you both to know how much this means to me, seeing that you're so serious about giving yourselves another try."

Chase frowned. "Well, we are, of course. But—"

"I'll accept whatever decision you reach, especially now that I see you're putting so much effort into this."

Annie and Chase stared at their daughter.

"Going off together, to Seattle. That's wonderful."

"Oh," Annie said, "but Dawn—"

"I had my doubts, you know? Whether you were really trying to work things out or if, well, if you were just trying to make me feel better." Dawn smiled. "Now I know, whatever happens, it's for real."

The loudspeaker crackled. "Last call for West Coast Air, Flight 606 to Seattle."

Dawn looped her arms through those of her parents.

"Come on," she said, "Nick and I will see you off."

"No," Annie said, rushing her words together, "really, kids, it isn't necessary."

But they were already marching across the lounge in lockstep, Annie on one side of Dawn, Chase on the other. When they reached the boarding gate, Dawn kissed them goodbye.

"I love you, Mom," she whispered as she pressed her cheek to Annie's.

"Dawn. Baby, you don't understand..."

"I do. And I know, in my heart, this is right."

"Folks?" Everyone looked up. The attendant at the gate was managing to smile and look stern at the same time. "Hurry, please, if you wish to make this flight."

"Chase?" Annie said desperately, as his hand closed over her elbow.

"Just walk," he muttered through his teeth, and steered her forward.

"No. This is impossible!"

"So is turning back. Walk, smile—and when we get on that plane, behave yourself."

"In your dreams, Cooper. Have you forgotten? I don't have a ticket."

Beside her, Chase made a sound that might have been a laugh.

"Sorry," he said, "but I'm afraid you do."

"Don't be silly! I have *your* ticket. I tried to tell you that."

Annie waved the envelope in his face, then went white as her ex-husband plucked an identical envelope from his jacket pocket.

"And I bought another one," he said. "I tried to tell *you* that."

"No," Annie whimpered.

"Yes."

Annie's feet felt as if they'd been nailed to the floor. Chase's hand tightened on her elbow.

"The clerk will notice the names! She'll see that I can't possibly be—"

Chase plucked the envelope from Annie's limp hand and yanked out the contents.

"Hurry," the attendant said, and the next thing Annie knew, she was seated beside him in the first-class cabin of a 747 as it lifted off into a bright, early-morning sky.

CHAPTER SIX

"I CANNOT BELIEVE THIS!"

Chase sighed, tilted back his seat and closed his eyes. Little men with hammers were dancing around inside his head, trying to beat their way out.

"I absolutely, positively cannot believe this!"

"So you've said, a hundred times this morning. Or maybe it was last night. I can't imagine why, but I seem to have lost track of time."

"To think I let you get me into this incredible mess—"

"Annie. Do us both a favor, will you? Lay off."

"—this *impossible* mess! And there you are, lying back with your eyes closed, relaxing, taking it easy, acting as if nothing out of the ordinary were happening!"

Chase's fingers tightened around the arms of his seat. Okay, she was upset. Upset enough so he could damn near feel her quivering with anger and indignation beside him but hell, he was upset, too.

He'd made a monumental screwup, lying to his daughter in the first place and now, as with most lies, he was getting in deeper and deeper. It didn't thrill him to know that, probably sooner than later, he was going to have to let his little girl down.

"Do you care? No. Uh-uh. You do not. No, sir, not Mr. Chase Cooper. He's as cool as a cucumber. He just sits there, as calm as he pleases!"

But first he was going to have to listen to Annie telling him what he already knew, that he was an idiot for having gotten them into this mess in the first place.

"—just drives me crazy! I'm sitting here, wound up like a spring, thinking about what a hideous mess we're in, but do you worry about it?"

"Annie, trust me. I'm worrying."

"You are not," Annie said coldly. "If you were worrying, you couldn't eat a mouthful. But you tore into your meal like a starving man at a banquet table."

"You're damned right I did. I was hungry. I haven't eaten a thing since the caterer fed me that tenderized shoe leather and slippery toadstool concoction at the wedding."

"Shoe leather? Toadstool?" Annie quivered with indignation. "That just shows what you know."

Chase looked at Annie. He thought of replying, then thought better of it. Hell, he thought wearily, she was right. What *did* he know?

Enough to have built Cooper Construction into what it was today—but not enough to have saved his own marriage. And now he, of all people, was trying to save his daughter's. There was a joke in there someplace, if only he could manage to see it.

He put his head back and let Annie's angry tirade wash over him. He was too tired to argue, or even to answer. He hadn't felt this exhausted since the early years of their marriage, when he'd spent his days working and his evenings taking courses in finance and administration and whatever else he'd figured might help him grow his business into something he and Annie could be proud of.

He could still remember coming home late at night, too tired to see straight—but not too tired to go into Annie's arms, or to sit across the kitchen table from her and talk about everything under the sun, from some problem at a job site to politics to Annie's day flipping burgers at the King.

When had it all started to go wrong? He'd tried and tried to figure it out, but there hadn't been any one day or any one event. Things had changed, that was all, little by little, and so subtly that even now, after all this time, he couldn't put his finger on it. He only knew that at some point, Annie had stopped waiting up for him.

Not while he was still in school. No, it was after that. When he was scrambling for jobs, taking on work two, three hours from home; he'd drive back at night, so worn-out he could barely make it, because he didn't want to be away from Annie...until he'd figured out that there wasn't any point because the only thing she'd say when she heard his key in the lock was "Don't track mud on the floor, Chase," and then she'd tell him his meal was in the microwave and she'd go off to bed.

Hours later, after he'd eaten his dried-out dinner and pored over plans and specs for the next day, he'd trudge upstairs and find her asleep or pretending to be, lying far over on her side of the mattress, her back to him, her spine so rigid he couldn't bring himself to touch her.

He'd thought things might improve when the money finally started coming in. He bought Annie extravagant gifts, things he'd always longed to give her, and sent her chocolates and huge bouquets of roses.

"Thank you," she'd say politely, and he'd feel as if he'd somehow failed her.

He'd still spent long hours on job sites—he was a hands-on kind of man, not the sort to sit behind a desk and anyway, if you wanted to stay on top of things, you had to be there, in the flesh. He knew he'd arrived when he began getting invited to all kinds of functions. Chamber of Commerce dinners. Charity affairs. Things he couldn't afford to turn down, because if you didn't network, some other guy would and then you'd lose the jobs you'd worked so hard to get—the jobs that bought the things he wanted Annie and Dawn to have. The things Annie had done without, for so long.

So he started accepting invitations. He didn't know how it would be, mingling with the doers and shakers; he was nervous, at first, and excited, but Annie was neither.

"Am I expected to go with you?" she asked, the first time he tossed a cream-colored charity ball announcement on the kitchen table.

Her response hurt. He'd still been foolish enough, in those days, to have hoped she'd get some pleasure at how he'd moved them up in the world.

"Yes," he'd said, speaking coldly to hide his disappointment. "You're my wife, aren't you?"

"Certainly," Annie had answered, and she'd gone out, bought a gown and all the stuff to go with it, had her hair done and sailed into the gilded hotel ballrooms and wood-paneled meeting rooms of their new life as if she'd never flipped hamburgers or burped a crying baby.

Lord, he'd been so proud of her. He'd been as nervous as a cat inside, wondering if he'd fit in, but not Annie. She'd brimmed with self-confidence. And she'd been so beautiful, so bright. He'd ached to keep her stapled to his side but he hadn't done it, not once he'd realized she didn't need him to shore her up. He knew how hard she'd worked in the background, all those years. It was little enough to do, to back off and let her shine on her own. Just as long as he was the guy who took her to the party and brought her home, he was happy.

What an idiot he'd been! It had turned out she'd hated spending those evenings with him. His first clue had come when she'd started saying no, she couldn't attend this function or that dinner because she'd signed up for some artsy-fartsy course that had no practical use except to make the very clear point that what she really wanted was a life apart from his.

He found himself devoting more time to business, spending days at a clip away from home. What did it matter? Dawn was slipping into her teenage years. Her life centered around her friends. As for Annie...Annie was never there. She was neck-deep in courses that only emphasized the growing differences between them.

How To Appreciate Haiku. Understanding Jasper Johns, whoever in hell Jasper Johns was. Batik-Making. And then, finally, what had seemed like a trillion courses in flower arranging and design and the next thing he'd known, he had a suitcase in his hand and it was goodbye, twenty years of marriage—well, there'd been that mess at the end that had finished things off, when his secretary had thrown herself into his arms, but he hadn't done a thing to encourage it, no matter what Annie thought.

Peggy had been lonely. As lonely as he was. Some quiet talk, a couple of suppers after they'd been poring over figures for hours in the office, followed by his seeing her into a taxi, never anything more personal than that. That was why nobody had been more surprised than he when Peggy had suddenly launched herself into his arms one night. And wouldn't you know that would be the one night in who knew how many years Annie had picked to come waltzing into the office?

Chase sighed. Not that it mattered anymore. He and Annie were long divorced. He'd made a new life for himself. A pleasant one and yes, he supposed—okay, he knew—that Janet would be delighted to be part of that life, if he asked her.

He'd been happy. Content.

Until today.

Until he'd taken Annie into his arms on that dance floor and felt things, remembered things, he didn't want to feel or remember. Until he'd opened his mouth and jammed his own big foot right into it. And now here he was, heading for Seattle, listening to Annie go on and on about what he'd done, and he had another couple of hours of listening ahead of him before their plane landed and he got her on a flight headed in the other direction.

"...could at least show some concern!"

Chase looked at his ex. Annie was staring straight ahead, her face flushed, her arms crossed over her middle.

"Listen," he said, "what would you like me to do? Get down on my knees and beg for forgiveness?"

She made a humphing sound and lifted her chin a notch.

"Maybe you want me to stand up and tell all these people what a chump I am."

Annie humphed again.

"Just tell me, all right? Say, 'Chase, here's what you've got to do if you want me to shut up.' And I'll do it, Annie, so help me, I'll do it, because I am tired unto death of listening to you bitch and moan!"

That got her attention. She swung toward him, her blue eyes flashing.

"Bitch and moan? Me?"

"Yes, you. Complain and nag, complain and nag, and all because I made one mistake."

"I am not complaining or nagging. I am merely stating the obvious. Yes, you made one mistake. A biggie. And now here we are, off on a trip to Portland—"

"Seattle."

"Dammit, what's the difference?"

"Portland's in Oregon. Seattle's in Washington. There's a big difference."

"Well, excuse me. I suppose I'd know the difference, if I had a college degree, but forgive me, I don't."

"Are you going completely nuts? What's a college degree got to do with this?"

What, indeed? Annie bit her lip. "Nothing."

"You're damn right," Chase said. "Now why don't you do us both a favor? Put back your seat, shut your eyes and try to get some rest."

"Oh, yes, that's easy for you to say but then, everything's easy for you to say! Otherwise, you'd never have gotten us into such a mess in the first place. How could you? How could you have told Dawn—"

"That's it," Chase said grimly, and he hauled Annie into his arms and kissed her. She was too surprised to fight him, and he took advantage of it, making the kiss long and deep. "Now," he said, drawing back just far enough so he could look straight into her eyes, "are you going to keep quiet? Because if you start babbling again, so help me, I'll kiss you until you shut up."

Annie's cheeks flooded with color.

"I hate you, Chase Cooper," she hissed.

Chase let her go. "What else is new," he said tiredly, and then he shut his eyes, told himself not to think about how good it had felt to kiss her because then he'd start remembering what making love had been like, before they'd turned away from each other, how it had been powerful and tender, wild and serene, and so much more than he'd ever imagined a basically simple physical act could be.

Stop it, he told himself angrily, and he tumbled into a deep, troubled sleep.

Annie watched with disgust as Chase slept beside her.

He was snoring softly, and from the look on his face she could tell that he was sleeping the sleep of the innocent.

Well, why be surprised? That was how he'd dealt with any kind of problem, before their divorce.

"By sleeping," she muttered, and scrunched down lower in her seat.

There'd been times, as soon as she'd realized their marriage was in trouble, when she'd spent half the day just thinking about what was going wrong, trying to put a name to it, to come up with an explanation and maybe a solution. Then she'd wait for Chase to come home, so they could talk.

What a slow learner she'd been!

How could you talk to a man who came dragging through the door hours late? Who pretended he'd been trudging around job sites or driving back from one when the simple truth was that he didn't come home because he had nothing to say to you anymore?

Was it her fault that she'd married him so young, before she'd had a chance to go to college, the way he had?

There'd been a brief time, after Cooper Construction had begun to grow, when she'd dared let herself dream that things were getting better.

But they hadn't. Things had gotten worse, instead, starting the night Chase had come home and told her, with a smug smile, that he'd been invited to a big-deal dinner. He wanted to go. It was, he'd said, a terrific opportunity.

He made it sound like an invitation to paradise.

"Do you want me to go?" she'd asked, and just for a minute, she'd looked into his eyes and prayed for him to say that all he really wanted was for them to love each other as they once had.

Instead he'd gotten a closed-up look on his face and said that she was his wife. Of course, he wanted her to go.

What he'd meant was that it was expected of her. Accompanying him to the party was part of her job description, like cooking the meals he never came home to share or warming his bed when he reached for her.

So she'd gone out and bought herself the right clothes, had her hair done the right way, and gone with him to the damned Chamber of Commerce party. Whatever. She couldn't really remember anymore. Not that it mattered. The dozen or more functions she'd attended on Chase's arm were all equally dull and dreary, and he didn't even stay with her during the evening. It was always the same. He'd introduce her, then go off on his own. Networking, not even making the slightest pretense that he enjoyed her company because the truth was, he didn't.

That was when she'd decided she was tired of playing the demure, domesticated backup to Chase's Captain of Industry. He had his degrees and his construction company; she could have something of her own, too.

An education. In things that would never interest him. He'd made that accusation, once, when he'd come home from a trip and she'd paused only long enough to acknowledge his presence before hurrying out the door to a lecture on haiku.

"Dammit," he'd roared, "is that how you pick courses from the catalog, Annie? Do you look the list over and say, hey, that's a good one! Maybe my big dumb husband won't even know what the name of the course means."

"However did you know?" she'd said with a chilly smile, and then she'd flounced out the door, but quickly, so that she wouldn't cry in front of him or say, Chase, please, what's happened to us? I love you. Tell me that you still love me.

It wasn't true, of course, about the courses. She took

the ones that sounded interesting: haiku because the description in the catalog sounded so spare and elegant. The one on Jasper Johns because one of Chase's clients had mentioned having a Johns collection, and the one on batik-making because she'd seen a dress in the window of a shop and been fascinated by the swirling colors.

She took the flower-arranging courses simply because there'd been a time in their lives when they were broke and desperately in love, and Chase had bought her a single red rose, because it was all he could afford, and she'd cherished it more than the huge bouquets that came, impersonally, by messenger once he'd struck it rich.

Oh, how much more wonderful that single rose had been!

He'd come home with it in his hand, years and years ago, along with wine and two tickets to the Virgin Islands, and when he'd offered her the rose he'd smiled shyly and said it was almost as beautiful as she was.

She could still remember how she'd gone into his arms.

"I'm sweaty, babe," he'd said huskily. "I need a shower."

And she'd said yes, he did, and she'd started to undress him, and a minute later they'd been naked, in the shower together.

Her skin tingled now, just remembering what it had been like, the long, slow soaping of each other's bodies, the kissing and touching, the way they'd ended up making love right there, under the spray, Chase's arms hard around her, her legs tight around his waist, him saying her name against her mouth, over and over, and she crying out as they came together in explosive release.

Tears stung behind her lids. It was stupid, thinking

about things like that. Especially about sex, because that brought her straight to what had finally ended their marriage.

She'd been taking a class in dried flower making and design. She'd done some nice work, she knew that, but one night the instructor had asked her to wait after she dismissed the class. Then she'd asked Annie's permission to enter one of her flower arrangements in a juried show.

Annie had said yes. And she'd been so happy and excited that she'd forgotten how long it had been since she and Chase had shared good news. She'd jumped into her car, driven to Chase's office building, found the front door unlocked and sailed down the hall, straight into his office...

Annie shuddered.

She could still see them now, her husband and his secretary, the girl with her arms around Chase's neck and his around her waist, their bodies pressed together...

That was it. The marriage was over.

Chase had tried to explain, to worm out of the truth, but Annie wasn't stupid. She'd endured enough pain, watching the man she loved slip slowly but steadily away from her all those years.

And "loved" was the right word. That night, as Chase and his secretary sprang guiltily apart, Annie knew that whatever she'd once felt for her husband was gone. Deader than a daffodil that's been squashed by a truck.

"Annie," Chase had said, "Annie, you have to listen."

"Yes, Mrs. Cooper," the young woman had pleaded, "you must listen!"

Listen? Why? There was nothing to talk about.

She'd felt suddenly very calm. The decision was out of her hands, thanks to Chase and the weeping girl.

"I want a divorce," she'd told him, and she'd even managed a cold smile for the secretary. "He's all yours," she'd said, and then she'd turned on her heel and marched out.

Things had gone quickly, after that. Her sister, Laurel, had recommended an attorney, although Laurel had done her best to convince Annie not to act so hastily. But there was nothing hasty in Annie's decision. She and Chase had been heading for this moment for years.

The divorce had been civilized. Chase's attorney was an old friend, David Chambers, who kissed her cheek and treated her with courtesy during their one face-to-face over a conference table. Chase wanted her to have the condominium. Half their savings. Half of everything. Child support, and generous alimony.

Annie said she didn't want the money. Her lawyer, and his, told her not to be stupid. She had a child to support. They were right, she knew, so she accepted everything except the alimony. As for the condo—it was filled with ugly memories. She sold it as soon as she could, moved to Stratham and began a new life. A career. She'd cut herself off from the past, and damned successfully. She'd made friends. She'd dated. And now she had Milton Hoffman, who wanted to marry her.

And then Chase had come along, spoiling everything with a stupid lie.

Annie chomped down on her lip.

Who was she kidding? Her life had started slipping off the tracks hours before Chase had told that dumb lie and the truth was, she understood that he'd done it not out of stupidity but out of love for their daughter.

The lie hadn't put her on this collision course with disaster.

The dance had. That silly dance at the wedding.

Annie tried not to remember. The warmth of Chase's

arms encircling her. The beat of his heart against hers. The feel of his lips against her hair, against her skin. The feeling that she had come home, that she was where she'd always belonged.

Oh God.

She took a long, shuddering breath.

Stop it, she told herself fiercely, and she put her head back, shut her eyes and willed herself to sleep.

A change of pitch in the jet's engines woke Chase hours later.

He yawned, tried to remember where he was—and went completely still.

Annie was asleep, with her head on his shoulder. She was tucked close against him, her face against his neck, just the way she used to back in the long-ago days when they'd cuddle up together on the sofa to watch Sunday football.

"You watch," she'd say, "I don't mind. I'll read."

But after a little while, she'd sigh. The book would slip from her hands. She'd put her head on his shoulder and sigh again, and he'd sit there with her asleep beside him, unwilling to move or to give up these sweet moments even if every muscle in his body ached.

A feeling of almost unbearable tenderness swept over him. She was dreaming, too. Looking down, into her face, he could see the little smile on her lips.

Was she dreaming about him?

"Annie?"

Annie sighed. "Mmm," she said.

"Babe, it's time to wake up."

She smiled and cuddled closer. "Mmm," she whispered, "Milton?"

Milton?

Milton Hoffman? That was the man in his wife's

dream? That was why she was smiling and cuddling up so close to him?

Chase felt his heart turn to ice.

Hoffman. That poor excuse for a man. That effete jerk. That was who Annie wanted. That was the kind of man she'd always wanted.

Why hadn't he seen it before?

Milton Hoffman, Professor of English, Shakespearean Authority and All-round Chrome Dome, never had mud on his wing tips. He never had to leave the house before dawn and come home, dragging his tail, long after dark. He never had to wonder if anybody noticed the shadow of dirt under his fingernails because ol' Milton had never had dirt under his fingernails, not in this lifetime.

Chase sat up straight. Annie's head bobbed; she made a little purring sound and nuzzled closer.

"Annie," he said coldly. "Wake up."

"Mmm."

Annie sighed. She was at that point where you know you're dreaming, but you're not quite ready to give up the dream. Not this dream. She was too interested in seeing how it would end.

She had been sitting in a classroom, with Milton on his knees beside her. He'd just proposed, and she was earnestly explaining why she had to turn him down.

I like you very much, Milton, she said, *and I respect you and admire you.*

But he wasn't Chase. His kisses had never stirred her the way Chase's did. His touch didn't set her on fire.

"Annie? Wake up."

"Milton," she said, and then she opened her eyes and saw Chase glaring at her from two inches away.

Annie jerked back, her face coloring. How long had she been asleep? How long had she been lying snuggled up against Chase as if she were a teenager in a drive-in theater—if there still were such places?

No wonder Chase was looking at her that way. God, she'd probably drooled all over him.

"Sorry." She put her hands to her hair and smoothed it back from her face. "I, ah, I guess I dozed off."

"And dreamed of Prince Charming," Chase said, with a tight little smile.

"Prince…?"

"Good old Milty. Your fiancé."

Annie stared at Chase and remembered her dream. "Did I—did I say anything?"

"What's the matter, Annie? Afraid I might have heard the dialogue that went with an X-rated dream?"

"It wasn't X-rated! I was just dreaming that—that…"

"Don't waste your breath." Chase's voice was chill. "I'm not interested."

Annie stiffened. "Sorry. I almost forgot. Nothing I ever had to say was of much interest to you, was it?"

"Mr. Cooper? Mrs. Cooper?" The flight attendant smiled down at them both. "We'll be landing in just a few minutes. Would you put your seat-backs up, please?"

"With pleasure," Chase said.

"I'm buying a return ticket the instant we touch down," Annie snapped, without looking at him.

"You won't have to. Believe me, it'll be my pleasure to buy you the ticket and to see you to the plane."

It was a fine idea. Unfortunately it didn't work.

The next plane to Boston was completely booked.

"Providence, then," Chase said. "Bradley…"

One by one, he rattled off the names of airports. One by one, the clerk at the ticket counter shook her head.

"We've had lengthy delays all morning," she said.

"Fog here, thunderstorms in the Midwest..." She smiled apologetically. "I might be able to get your wife—"

"Ex-wife," Annie said.

"Whatever. I might be able to get her out of here tomorrow afternoon."

"Yeah," Chase grumbled, "okay."

"Not okay!" Annie glared at him, as if it was his fault she was in this predicament. "What am I supposed to do until tomorrow afternoon? Sit around the airport?"

"I'll get you a hotel room."

"Good luck."

Annie and Chase looked at the ticket clerk, whose shoulders rose and fell in a helpless shrug.

"On top of all the delays, there're two major conventions in town." She leaned forward and lowered her voice to a confidential whisper. "My boss tried everything he knew to get a room for a VIP just a little while ago, and even he couldn't come up with anything."

Annie had a mental picture of herself joining the rows of exhausted travelers draped over every available seat in the terminal.

"Don't worry," Chase said quickly. "I'm sure my client's arranged a room somewhere for me. You can have it just as soon as I get in touch with him."

As if in response, an electronically amplified voice rang out, paging Mr. Chase Cooper.

Chase took Annie's arm, drew her aside and picked up a courtesy phone.

"Yes?" He listened, then sighed and rolled his eyes as if to say this was just one more problem he didn't need. "Mr. Tanaka," he said politely. "No, no, I didn't see your man holding up my name at the arrivals gate." He glared at Annie, who glared right back. "I was, ah, preoccupied."

"Who is it?" Annie hissed.

Chase turned away. "Well, that's very kind of you, Mr. Tanaka. Sending a car for me…thank you."

"Is it somebody from Seattle?" Annie said, dancing in front of him. "Ask him if he knows of a hotel that might have a room."

Chase sighed. She was right. Kichiro Tanaka, his new client, was a wealthy and well-connected businessman. He had major investments in the southwest, and now he'd turned his attention to the coast. For all Chase knew, the guy might even own a hotel in this city.

"Mr. Tanaka… Yes, I'll meet your driver at the exit. In just a moment. But first—I wonder if you might be able to help me out with a small problem?"

Annie's mouth thinned. That's what she was, all right. A small problem. It was all she'd ever been, as far as Chase was concerned.

"Well…" Chase rubbed the back of his neck. "My, ah, my wife accompanied me to Seattle."

"Ex-wife," Annie snapped.

Chase glared at her and slapped his hand over the mouthpiece of the phone.

"Do you really want me to start explaining what you're doing here to a stranger?"

Annie colored. After a second, Chase cleared his throat and spoke again.

"She didn't intend to stay, though. Yes, well, I suppose that's one way of looking at it."

"What is?" Annie demanded.

"Charming. Yes. Yes, that she'd fly all this distance, just so we could spend a few hours more together."

Annie opened her mouth, stuck the tip of her finger inside and pretended to gag.

"The problem, Mr. Tanaka, is that all the flights have been delayed. It's probable Annie won't be able to leave until tomorrow and I've been told all the hotels are solidly booked… Really?''

''Really, what?'' Annie said.

''That's fine. Yes, of course. At the exit area, in a couple of minutes. Thank you, sir. I'll…we'll see you soon.''

''What?'' Annie said again.

Chase hung up the phone and grabbed her hand.

''Come on. We've got to meet the car and driver he sent for me.''

''Hot stuff,'' she muttered. ''A car and a driver, all for you.''

''And a suite, all for us.'' His smile was quick and shiny. ''So stop complaining.''

Annie looked at him as they hurried toward the escalator.

''You mean…?''

''I mean, luckily for you, he says there's more than enough room for the both of us.''

''Not in one hotel room, there isn't.''

''Didn't you hear what I said?'' They'd reached the lower level, and Annie hurried to keep up with Chase's long stride. ''He says we'll have a living room, bedroom, kitchen and bathroom all to ourselves.''

''Well, that's good news,'' Annie snapped, as Chase thrust her out the door ahead of him.

''Damn right. The last thing I feel like doing is curling up in a hotel lobby tonight while you take over my bed.''

''Such gallantry. But—''

''But what?'' Chase snapped in her ear as a black limousine slid to the curb. The driver got out, executed a perfect salute and opened the rear door. ''Just get into the car, Annie. We can endure each other's company a little while longer. As tempting at the thought of leaving you at the airport is, I can't bring myself to do it.''

As tempting as it was, staying at the airport for end-less hours didn't appeal to her, either.

"All right," she snapped back. "But you better hope this suite is the size of Yankee Stadium. Otherwise, you may find yourself sleeping in the lobby anyway!"

It wasn't the size of Yankee Stadium—although it was close.

But it wasn't a suite, Annie thought an hour later, as she stared around her in shock. And it certainly wasn't a hotel.

The limo had not taken them to one of the high-rise buildings in downtown Seattle. It had whisked them to a pier, where they'd boarded a sleek motorboat.

"Chase," Annie had said, over the roar of the boat's engines, "where are we going?"

Chase, who'd been starting to think he knew the an-swer, looked at the pilot.

"Tell me that we aren't going to the island," he said.

The pilot grinned. "Sure enough, we are."

Chase groaned.

Annie looked at him as he gripped the railing and stared out over the churning water. She'd read the one, silent word on his lips and the tips of her ears had turned pink.

Now, standing in this room, she half wanted to say the word herself.

The wisps of fog that had drifted across the boat's bow during their journey had lifted as they'd neared their destination. Annie had glimpsed an island, a place of towering green trees sloping down to a rocky shore. High among the trees, as if it were an eagle soaring out over the water, there was a lodge. It was a magnificent sight, a sculpture of redwood and glass. It was a fabulous aerie, commanding a view of the Sound in isolated splendor.

Wooden steps led up the craggy face of the cliff. Annie had climbed them, refusing Chase's outstretched hand and instead clasping the wooden railing, telling herself that when they reached the top, she'd see something more than that one structure. A hotel. A cluster of buildings. A resort...

But there was only the lodge, and when Chase opened the door and went inside, she followed.

The rooms they passed through were spectacular. There was a kitchen, white and shiny and spotless. A bathroom, complete with a deep Jacuzzi and a stall shower built against a glass wall so that it seemed open to the forest. There was a living room and as Annie stepped into it, sunlight suddenly poured through the huge skylight overhead, so that the white walls and pale hardwood floor seemed drenched in gold.

Mr. Tanaka's ancient heritage showed in the room's elegant yet simple lines: the woven tatami mats on the floor, the handsome shoji screen that served as a backdrop for a low, black-lacquered table and the plump, black-and-white silk cushions that were strewn on the floor before the fieldstone fireplace. Sliding glass doors, flanked by tall white vases filled with pussy willows, opened on to the deck.

But it was the bedroom that made Annie gasp, and mentally repeat Chase's muttered profanity. Their absent host's living room had been serenely Japanese—but Mr. Tanaka had very Western tastes when it came to his sleeping quarters.

The floor was covered with white carpet so deep and lush it made Annie's toes curl longingly inside her sneakers. One wall was mirrored; one was all glass and gave out onto the forest and the Sound. The furnishings themselves were spare and handsome. There was a teak dresser. A matching chest. A bentwood rocking chair.

And a bed.

One enormous, circular bed, elevated on a platform beneath a hexagonal skylight, and swathed in yards and yards of black-and-white silk.

CHAPTER SEVEN

ANNIE TOLD HERSELF to calm down.

Count to ten. To twenty. Concentrate on finding the peaceful center within herself. Wasn't that what she'd spent six weeks trying to learn when she'd taken that Zen philosophy course last winter?

Take a deep breath. Hold it. One. Two. Three. Four.

Annie let out her breath. It wasn't working. All she could see was the bed. All she could think about was Chase, standing next to her with a look of bland innocence on his face.

"Damn," she said, and when that clearly wasn't going to be anywhere near enough to relieve her anger, she gave up Zen for reality, swung around and punched her ex-husband in the belly. It was a hard belly—he'd always had a great body, and apparently that hadn't changed, which somehow only made her more furious— and she felt the jolt of the blow shoot straight up her arm and into her shoulder. But it was worth it to see the look of shock that spread across his face.

"Hey," he said, dancing back a step. Not that Annie's reaction entirely surprised him. She looked as if she could have happily murdered him. Well, hell, he understood that. He'd have happily murdered good old Kichiro Tanaka, given the opportunity. "Hey, take it easy, will you?"

"Take it easy?" Annie slapped her hands on her hips and glared at him, her chest rising and falling with each quick, huffy breath. "Take it easy?" she repeated, her voice shooting out of its normal range into a ragged soprano.

"Yeah." Chase rubbed his midsection. "There's no need to get violent over what's obviously a mistake."

"Oh, it's a mistake, all right." She blew a breath that lifted the curls dangling over her eyes. "A big mistake, Cooper, because if you think, even for one minute, that I—that you and I—that the two of us are going to share that—that bed, that we're going to relive old times—"

"Babe..."

"Don't 'babe' me!"

"Annie, you don't think..."

"But I do. I think. I always have, even though you never credited me for having a brain in my head when we were married."

Chase almost groaned. Here they went again, plunging right into deep water.

"Listen," he said carefully, "I know you're upset. But—"

"That's it. Tell me I'm upset. That way, I'll shut my mouth and you won't have to listen to the truth."

"Annie..."

"Let me tell you something, Chase Cooper. That might have worked years ago, but not now. I am not the dumb little thing you always thought I was."

"Annie, I never thought—"

"Yes, you did, but it doesn't matter a damn anymore."

"I swear, I didn't."

"'Oh, *Ba-aabe*,'" she said, cruelly mimicking his voice, "'I'm so sorry, but you don't mind if I go out, do you? I've got to attend a meeting of the—the Sacred Sons of the Saxophones tonight.'"

Despite himself, Chase laughed. "The what?"

"Don't try and joke your way out of this, Cooper!"

Annie took a step forward, her index finger uplifted and wagging an inch off his nose. "You can't change the facts."

"What facts?"

"I'm talking about our so-called marriage, that's what! And how you used to treat me as if I never had a thought in my head."

"I still don't know what the hell you're talking about!"

"Well, let me refresh your memory. Think back to the good old days, when you used to drag me to all those horrible dinners and charity things."

"Like the Sacred Sons of the Saxophones?"

"I just said, don't try and laugh your way out of this, Chase. I am dead serious."

"About what?"

She had to give him credit; he'd managed to put on an expression of total bewilderment. If she hadn't known better, she'd have thought he meant it.

"I know how you worried that your poor little wifey wouldn't be able to hold her own."

"What?"

"And then, when it turned out I could, you just—just left me, dumped me into a—a seaful of sharks and took off by yourself."

"Annie, you're crazy. I never—"

"Was that when you looked around and decided you could have lots more fun if you left me at home?"

Chase's expression went from bewilderment to confusion. "One of us is losing her mind," he said, very calmly. "And it sure as hell isn't me."

Annie's chin rose pugnaciously. "Hah," she said, and folded her arms.

"You think I was glad when you stopped going to

those dinners and things with me, so I could go by myself and have a wild old time?''

"You said it, not me.''

"Damn, but your spin on ancient history is truly amazing!''

"What's the matter, Chase? Can't you stand the truth?''

"Am I supposed to have forgotten that I stopped taking you with me because you made it clear how much you hated going?''

Annie flushed. "Don't try and twist things. Okay, maybe I didn't care for those stuffy evenings—''

"Finally, the woman speaks the truth!''

"Why would I have enjoyed them? We were only there so you could grab yourself another headline in the business section of the newspaper!''

Chase's eyes narrowed. "We were there so I could land myself jobs, Annie. Jobs, remember? The stuff that put bread on the table?''

"Give me a break, Chase! We had plenty of money by then. You were just—just getting your ego stroked.''

A muscle knotted in his cheek.

"Go on,'' he said softly. "What else have you saved up, all these years?''

"Only that when I finally said I didn't want to go anymore, instead of trying to change my mind, which any intelligent man would have done, which *you* would have done, at one time—''

Chase gave a short, desperate laugh. "Are we both speaking the same language here, or what?''

"Instead of doing that,'' Annie said, ignoring the interruption, "you simply shrugged your shoulders and agreed. And that was that.''

"You're telling me that I should have tried to talk you into doing something you obviously hated?''

"Don't make it sound as if you don't understand a word I'm saying, Chase. I won't buy it."

"And I won't buy you making me into some kind of Neanderthal who cheered when my wife signed off and let me go play with the rest of the boys," Chase said grimly. "No way, babe, because that's *not* how it was, no matter what you say!"

"Yeah, well, that's your story and you're stuck with it."

"No!" Chase grabbed her wrist as she started past him. "No, it damn well is not 'my story.' It's fact. Did you expect me to get down on my knees and beg you to spend your evenings with me, instead of with one dumb textbook after another?"

"Right. Lay everything off on me, even my wanting to better myself. That's typical. Everything was my fault, never yours."

"Better yourself? *Better* yourself?" he said, bending toward her, his eyes dark and dangerous. "So that you could do what, huh? Tell me that you knew more about haiku than I knew about building houses?"

"That's not the way it was and you know it," Annie said angrily, as she tried to pull her arm from his grasp. "You couldn't bear to see me turning into a whole person instead of just being Mrs. Chase Cooper."

"Wasn't being my wife enough to make you happy?"

"Being the woman who cooked your meals and cleaned your house and raised your child, you mean," Annie said, her voice trembling. "Who waited up nights while you built your empire. Who got told to buy fancy dresses and jewelry so she could be dragged to Chamber of Commerce meetings as a reflection of her husband's importance!"

Chase could feel a humming in his ears. He let go of Annie's wrist and took a step back.

"If that's what you believe," he said, his voice so low and dangerous that it made the hair lift on the back of Annie's neck, "if you really think that's what you meant to me, my once-upon-a-time-wife, then it's a damn good thing our marriage ended when it did."

Annie stared at his white face and pinched lips. "Chase," she said, and held out her hand, but it was too late. He'd already whirled away from her and disappeared down the hall.

Unbelievable!

Chase walked along the gravel path that led from the lodge into the trees.

It was more than unbelievable. It was incredible, that Annie should have hated him so. Hated being married to him, and for so many years.

He tucked his hands into his pockets and slowed his pace, scowling at a squirrel that scolded him from beneath the branches of a cedar.

He knew a lot of guys who'd been divorced. They were everywhere: at his health club, at the board meetings he sat in on…it seemed as if you couldn't throw a stick in New York or San Francisco or any city in the whole U.S.A. without hitting some poor bastard who'd gone from being a family man to being a guy who thought a microwave meal was gourmet dining.

The happy bachelor image, the divorced stud with a little black book full of names and addresses, was the stuff of movies. It wasn't reality or if it was, then he'd missed something. The divorced men he met were almost invariably just like him, guys who'd once had it all and now had nothing but questions.

When had it all started to go wrong? And why? And then there was the biggest question of all.

What could they have done to change it?

Most of them had answers, even if they didn't much like them. Chase never had. Try as he would, he'd never really been able to pinpoint when things had started going downhill, or why. As for changing it…how could you change something when you didn't know what it was that needed changing?

He'd been the best kind of husband he'd known how to be, working his butt off to give Annie a better life. A life she deserved, and now it turned out she'd not only hated all the years of hard work, but she'd also resented them.

A bitter taste filled his mouth.

"What does she think?" he muttered, kicking a pine-cone out of the way. "Does she think I enjoyed working like a slave? Does she think I had a good time, busting my backside all day and cracking books half the night?"

Maybe. Annie had just proved that she was capable of thinking damn near anything, when it came to him.

The land was sloping upward. The trees were pressing in from either side, and a cool, salt-scented breeze was blowing into his face. Chase drew it deep into his lungs, lowered his head and trudged on.

At least it was all out in the open, now. Annie had been as remote about their split-up as the sphinx. He couldn't even remember which of them had said the words first, he or she; he only knew that except for that one awful scene at the end, when Annie had come bursting into his office and seen poor Peggy embarrassing them both—except for that, their separation had been the most civilized thing on record.

No harsh words. No screaming matches. No accusations. Nothing. They had both been polite and proper about the whole thing. His attorney had even joked about it.

"I had a law prof used to say that the only man who

never raises his voice during divorce proceedings is a
man whose almost-ex-wife's already slit his throat,"
David had said, and Chase had grinned and said that
David, with his own strikeout, certainly ought to know.

Chase shook his head. No, Annie hadn't killed him
when she'd thought she'd caught him being unfaithful.
She'd waited, and let him suffer for five long years, and
now she'd plunged a dagger right into his heart.

It shouldn't have hurt, not when she wasn't his wife
anymore. Not when she didn't mean a damn thing to
him anymore.

Chase stepped out of the woods. He was standing on
a high, rocky cliff overlooking the dark green Pacific.

Who was he kidding? Annie meant everything to him.
She always had, and she always would.

Annie sat on the edge of the circular bed, her hands
folded in her lap.

Well, she'd finally gotten everything out of her system. She'd let it all hang out; wasn't that what the kids
used to say? She'd dredged up all the anger and pain
she'd thought was long gone and dumped it right into
Chase's lap.

She sighed, fell back against the pillows and put her
arm over her eyes.

Who was she kidding? Neither the hurt nor the rage
was long gone. They weren't gone at all. Hardly a week
went by that something didn't make her remember how
miserable her marriage had been, how much she'd despised Chase.

It was just a good thing she'd finally gotten it out in
the open.

Tears welled in her eyes.

It wasn't true. Her marriage hadn't been miserable.
Not the first years, anyway. She'd been so crazy in love,

so happy, that sometimes she'd had to pinch herself to make sure she wasn't dreaming.

And she'd never despised Chase. Heaven knew, that would have made things a lot easier. Then, when she'd finally acknowledged the truth, that he'd outgrown her and that he didn't love her anymore, it wouldn't have hurt so badly.

Annie sighed, stood up, and walked to the window wall. The view was spectacular: the deep green water in one direction, and a stand of windblown cypresses stretching off in the other. The ancient trees looked as if they'd been there forever, protecting the house and keeping it safe.

A smile moved across her lips.

That was how she'd always felt about Chase. They'd met so young that there were moments she'd felt as if she'd known him all her life. And her safe haven had always been within his arms.

It had come as a shock to her to learn that other women didn't feel that way about their husbands. She could still recall sitting on a bench at a little playground years ago. Dawn must have been two, maybe three; she was playing with a bunch of kids and the mothers sat around watching, keeping an eye on things while they chatted about this and that.

Eventually the talk had turned to husbands.

"He drives me nuts," one woman said, "coming in the door at night like some kind of conquering hero, and I'm supposed to hum a couple of bars of Hail to the Chief while I pull off his shoes, stoke the fire and serve him a meal straight out of *Gourmet* magazine."

There'd been some laughter, some groans and lots of general agreement. Annie had been too flustered to do much of anything except sit there and think how sad it was that all those women didn't feel as she did, waiting for the sound of her husband's key in the lock so that she could fly into his arms.

Her throat tightened. She leaned her head forward and pressed her forehead against the cool glass.

When had it all started to change? When had eager anticipation turned to annoyance? When had the clock on the wall become not a way to count off the minutes and hours until Chase's arrival but an infuriating reminder of his lateness?

All the things she'd just said to him...how long had they been waiting to come out?

She'd hurt him, she knew. But he'd hurt her, too. Dragging her to those business affairs, with her all gussied up to prove his success.

That was the way it had been, wasn't it?

Wasn't it?

And he'd said such awful things just now. Implying that she'd studied stuff just so she could show him his ignorance of the fine arts...

Annie snorted and turned her back to the window. What a lie! She'd never done that. How could she? Chase was the one with the college degrees; she was the meek little wife with nothing but a high school diploma. It wasn't her fault if she'd taken an interest in obscure poetry and Indonesian art and things that were beyond his comprehension...

Things that were beyond his comprehension.

She drew a deep, shuddering breath.

No. Never. She wouldn't have studied anything for such a shabby reason. She'd enjoyed the poetry, the art; she'd improved herself with the vocabulary courses and the Great Books series, and if Chase just happened to be overwhelmed by the books she left open on the kitchen table, it wasn't anything deliberate on her part.

A muffled sob burst from Annie's throat.

"I never meant to hurt you, Chase," she whispered. Never.

She'd loved him, with all her heart. She loved him still. That was the awful truth of it, and there wasn't a damn thing she could do about it now because he didn't love her, not anymore.

Their marriage was over. Chase was engaged to another woman, and she—she was going to have to go on without him.

It was just that it was going to be harder, now.

It was always harder, once you knew the truth.

Chase knocked on the open bedroom door.

"Come in," Annie said politely.

He stepped into the room.

She was sitting in the rocker, her hands folded neatly in her lap. Her face was pale but her features were composed, and she smiled when she saw him.

"Hi."

"Hi."

"Did you go for a walk?"

"Yeah, I did." He hesitated. "Listen, about all that stuff we said before. I'm really sorry—"

"Me, too. There's no reason to quarrel over the past."

Chase nodded. "No reason at all."

They smiled at each other, and then Annie cleared her throat. "So," she said briskly, "I'll bet the island's beautiful."

"It is. I was here before. Tanaka bought the place from some computer megamillionaire. He flew me out to see it after he'd signed the papers. He wanted to know what I thought of his plan."

"What plan?" Annie asked politely.

"He's going to tear this place down, build a kind of retreat."

"Ah." She looked down, and plucked a bit of thread off her jeans-clad leg. "Buddhist?"

Chase smiled. "Top-class hotel, would be closer to the mark. What he's got in mind is a kind of hideaway for his executive staff. You know the sort of thing— elegant but rustic. Simple food, prepared by a Cordon Bleu chef. Simple suites, with a Jacuzzi in every bathroom and a wet bar in every sitting room. Simple pleasures, starting with a nine-hole golf course, tennis courts and an Olympic-size swimming pool."

"A bigger, even more elaborate version of this, you mean."

"Yeah." Chase grinned. "Incredible, isn't it?"

"Incredible's the word, all right. So, you're going to build this Shangri-la for him?"

"Well, not quite the way he'd envisioned it, no. I told him that he'd ruin the feeling of the land and the sea, if he went overboard on the luxuries."

"No wet bars?"

Chase grinned. "And no suites, no golf courses, no tennis courts, and why put in a pool when Puget Sound's outside your door?"

"That's darned near a pool in the bathroom already," Annie said, smiling. "Heaven knows, it's too big for just one pers..." Color swept into her face. Her eyes met Chase's, and she looked quickly away. "I'll, uh, I'll bet you had a tough time, convincing him."

Chase shrugged. "Well, it took a while, yes."

Silence filled the room. Finally Annie spoke.

"Chase?"

"Yes?"

"Well...well..." She took a deep breath. "Listen, I know it'll be embarrassing for you to have to admit to your Mr. Tanaka that you and I ended up in the plane together by mistake, but you're going to have to do it.

Tell him anything you want. Whatever's easiest for you. Lay it off on me, if you like. Say that I suddenly thought of something important back home.''

"Your fiancé," Chase said politely. "I could say you forgot about him. How's that sound?"

Annie refused to acknowledge the gauntlet, much less stoop to pick it up.

"I don't care what you say. Just—just get me off this island, please."

Chase nodded. She was right. They both needed to leave this place. "I'll take care of it."

"You could tell him the same thing," Annie blurted as he turned toward the door. He looked at her, and she ran the tip of her tongue over her lips. "You know," she said, because it was too late to back down, "that you have to get back to your fiancée, too."

Chase looked at his ex-wife. Sitting on the edge of the rocker, ankles crossed, hands locked together, with the rays of the late-afternoon sun streaking her hair with gold, she looked soft, sweet and undescribably vulnerable. He saw himself going to her, taking her in his arms, kissing her and telling her that she was the only woman he'd ever wanted, the only woman he'd ever loved.

"Chase?"

"Yeah," he said gruffly. "Uh, the thing is—we've both forgotten something."

"I don't think so," Annie said, fighting against the tears that inexplicably threatened. "Believe me, Chase, we haven't forgotten a thing."

"No flight back until tomorrow, babe. No hotel rooms, either."

"Oh." Annie chewed on her lip. "Well, that's okay. I'll wait at the airport."

"That's not a good idea."

"It's a fine idea." Annie smiled brightly. "I've always liked airports. I can buy myself half a dozen magazines and a hot dog, curl up in a corner and—''

''Listen, we'll stay right where we are. But we'll start over. New ground rules. No talking about the past, or about us. Okay?''

''The past, and us, are the only things we've got,'' Annie said quietly. ''I don't see how we can avoid talking about them.''

Chase looked at her for a long moment. Then he sighed and ran his fingers through his hair.

''I'll go find the guy who brought us here. He can take us back to shore. And I'll phone Tanaka and see if he can pull some strings to get you a room somewhere. Or I'll stay with you at the airport, until you can get a flight out.''

''That won't be necessary.''

''Look, we can argue about it later. Right now, let me just put the wheels in motion.''

''What'll you tell him? Your Mr. Tanaka? About why we want to leave the island, I mean?''

His mouth twisted. ''Don't start worrying about how I handle business at this late date, Annie. It's my problem, not yours.''

Chase strode from the room and slammed the door after him. Annie sat back in the rocker. She was shaking, and she felt like crying, which was stupid. It only proved how much pressure she'd been under, the last couple of days.

She took a deep breath, heel-and-toed the rocker into motion and settled in to wait for her liberation from this island, Chase, and a thousand unwanted memories.

''He's gone.''

Annie blinked her eyes open and swung her legs to the floor.

"Who?" she said, in a hoarse voice. She frowned and rubbed her hands over her eyes. "Who's gone?"

Chase leaned back against the wall and folded his arms. His face looked as if it had been chipped from granite.

"The guy who brought us here."

Annie's head was swimming. "I'm not—I'm not following you. The guy with the boat, you mean?"

"Uh-huh."

"How can he be gone? *Where* could he have gone? He couldn't have walked to…" Her breath caught at the expression on Chase's face. "You mean, he took the boat?"

"You've got it."

Annie stared at him. "We're stuck here?"

"Right again."

"Well—well, phone your Mr. Tanaka. Tell him—"

"Will you stop calling him that? He is *not* my Mr. Tanaka." Chase glowered at her. "Anyway, I already tried to phone him."

"And?"

"And," he said, shrugging his shoulders, "it's not a regular phone they've got here, it's a radio thing."

"So?"

"So, it doesn't seem to work."

Annie bit her lip and fought down a rising tide of hysteria. "If this is your idea of some kind of joke, Chase…"

"Do I look like I'm joking?" Chase smiled tightly. "The guy left a note, in the kitchen. It seems we're trapped until tomorrow."

"That's impossible. Why would he strand us here?"

"I don't know why. I don't much care, either. All I know is that we're going to have to make the best of things, until the jerk with the boat shows up tomorrow morning at eight.''

"At eight," Annie repeated, through lips that felt numb. She looked at her watch. Sixteen hours to get through. Sixteen hours, alone with her ex-husband.

"Just get this through your head," Chase said. Annie looked up. "This setup. This—this honeymoon hotel. I assure you, it wasn't my idea."

"I certainly hope not. Because if it was, you're in for a heck of a disappoint—"

Annie gasped as Chase grabbed her shoulders and hauled her to her feet.

"Lady, I have taken all the insults I'm going to take! I promise you, I'm not so desperate for a woman to warm my bed that I'd go to all this trouble to arrange it."

He was right, and she knew it. Her accusation had been dumb. He couldn't have arranged this fiasco if he'd wanted to.

And he was right about all the rest, as well. Chase wouldn't have to resort to subterfuge, to get a woman into his bed. He was—what had Deb called him, the day of the wedding? Hunky, that was it. He was hunky and he always had been, especially now that he was in his prime. Chase was a man who'd turn women's heads without even trying.

No wonder she spotted his photo in the paper so often, with some smiling bimbo on his arm.

Except they weren't bimbos. She might as well admit that, too, while she was going for the truth. She liked to tell herself they were, but the women in the photos with her ex-husband were invariably beautiful and elegant.

Like Janet Pendleton, who was going to become his wife.

Annie's throat felt raspy. It was silly, but she felt like crying.

"You're right," she said.

"You're damned right I am."

"This entire thing—our getting on that plane in the first place, and now our getting stuck here is—just, what's the word? Karma."

Chase could hardly believe it. Annie, holding out an olive branch? It seemed inconceivable but hell, most of what had happened during the past forty-eight hours fell into that very same category. If it was an olive branch, what did he have to lose if he accepted it? If he was going to spend the night in that rocker—and he was—it would be a lot better for the both of them if they weren't at each other's throats.

"Karma," he said, as he lifted his hands from her shoulders. "Don't tell me. You're taking a course in Eastern religions."

Annie smiled and shook her head. "I bought a computer. That's what the guy who installed it said. It's karma if you can get a computer to work right, and karma if you can't."

"You bought yourself a computer?"

"For business. But it's turned out to be fun, too. The Internet, that kind of thing."

"Uh-huh. Who showed you how to use it? The pan...Hoffman?"

"I taught myself. Well, with a little help from Dawn."

"Really." Chase smiled. "Maybe you'll give me some pointers, sometime. I'm still all thumbs at anything more complicated than punching up a spreadsheet."

"Sure."

Their eyes met and held, and then Chase made a show of looking around at the room. "I'm really sorry about this. The accommodations, I mean. I never dreamed Tanaka would dump us out here.''

"It's a bit much, I admit." Annie smiled. "But it's beautiful, too. Maybe this is what hotels are like, wherever it is he comes from.''

Chase grinned. "He's from Dallas, babe—I mean, Annie. No, I suspect he figured we wanted to spend some private time together.''

Annie laughed. "Cupid Tanaka, huh?''

"So it would seem.''

Again, silence closed around them. Annie sat down on the edge of the rocker.

"So," she said briskly, "what're you going to do? Tear this place down, then build the retreat he wants from scratch?''

"Something like that.''

"I'll bet the final result will be spectacular.''

"Livable, anyway," Chase said, leaning back against the wall and folding his arms.

Annie smiled. "Don't be modest, Chase. I know your work is well thought of. I see your name—the company's name—in the papers all the time. You've made it to the top.''

"So they tell me." His tone was flat, and so was his smile. "To tell you the truth, the only thing I've noticed is that if that's where I am, it's not all it's cracked up to be.''

"Aren't you happy?''

"Are you?''

She stared at him. Why was she hesitating? Of course, she was happy. She had her house. Her business. Friends. Interests. A life that was comfortable, not one in which she was expected to play a role.

"Annie?''

She looked up. Chase had moved closer. She had only to reach out her hand, if she wanted to touch him.

"Are you happy?" he asked softly.

She wanted to say that she was. To tell him what she'd just told herself, how her life had taken on shape and meaning.

Instead she found herself thinking how wonderful it had felt when they'd kissed. She wanted to tell him that though she'd made a good life for herself, there was an emptiness to it that she hadn't even been aware of until she'd gone into his arms on the dance floor.

But to say any of that would have been stupid. Chase was out of her life; she was out of his. That was the way they both wanted it. Hadn't they proved that a few hours ago, when they'd gone at each other, hammer and tong? Whatever she thought she'd felt since the wedding was an aberration.

"Yes," she said, with a smile that felt as if it were stretching her lips grotesquely, "certainly, I'm happy. I've never been more content in my life."

A curtain seemed to drop over Chase's eyes.

"Of course," he said politely. "You're happy, with your business and your fiancé."

Annie nodded. "And so are you."

"Yeah. And so am I."

They looked at each other and then Chase walked to the door.

"Well," he said briskly, "I think I'll go check out the refrigerator. There's bound to be enough food for a couple of meals there, or in the freezer."

"All the conveniences, hmm? Even way out here."

"Everybody's got a different definition of roughing it, I guess."

"So I see. If you'd told me we'd end up in a cabin on an island a million miles from civilization, I'd have imagined a one-room shack with a propane stove on the porch and an outhouse in the back.''

Chase smiled. "Like the place we rented that summer after we got married. Remember? The outdoor sun-shower, the one-hole, no-flush john…"

Annie laughed. "How could I forget? We bought that funny set of pots and pans that were supposed to fit inside each other, and those sleeping bags…"

"Boy, we were dumb," Chase said, laughing, too. "We must have spent, what, an hour or more trying to figure out how to zip the bags together because we sure as hell weren't going to sleep apart…" His words trailed off. "Damn," he said softly, "I haven't thought of that weekend in years."

Neither had Annie. Just remembering made her throat constrict.

"I—I think I'll go freshen up," she said. "And then—and then, maybe I'll take a walk, too. Just to clear my head. The flight was so long, and—and everything's been so hurried…"

"Yeah. Sure." Chase swallowed dryly. "You go on. Wash up, walk around, whatever. I'll check out the supplies."

"I'll come give you a hand in a few minutes." She gave a quick, brittle laugh. "I wish I had a hairbrush with me, or even some lipstick. I feel like a complete mess."

Chase thought of telling her the truth, that she didn't need a brush or cosmetics because she was already more beautiful than any woman he'd ever known.

Hell, he thought, and he pulled open the door, stepped out into the hall and strode away from temptation as fast as he could without breaking into a run.

CHAPTER EIGHT

CHASE GLANCED at his watch.

The Tanaka Hotel wasn't as perfect as it looked, he thought wryly. The freezer and the refrigerator had turned out to be surprisingly empty. Someone must have emptied things out, in preparation for the day the cabin would be demolished.

Still, there'd been some usable stuff in the pantry and he'd been able to come up with the makings for an improvised meal. Now, he was peeling potatoes and onions but his thoughts were elsewhere. Fifteen minutes had gone by since he'd heard the front door open, then shut as Annie had gone off on her walk.

Maybe he ought to go look for her.

Not that there was anything to worry about on this island. It was wild and isolated, but nothing here could harm her. There were no predatory animals, not of a size to be a problem. No bears, or coyotes…

Well, he supposed there probably were snakes, though the odds of Annie meeting up with one on the neatly kept gravel path that traversed the island were remote.

Spiders, though. There were definitely spiders—he'd seen some Class A specimens the first time Tanaka had brought him out here. They'd been the size of a child's fist but they were harmless.

It was just that Annie had a thing about creepy crawlies.

He'd learned that the winter he'd scored his first really big contract. On his way home after he'd landed the deal, he'd stopped to buy Annie a box of chocolates. There was a kid on the corner near the subway, selling single red roses; Chase had selected the prettiest one he could find and just then, he'd spied a travel agency across the street. There was a big, bright poster in the window.

Come To The Virgin Islands, it said.

Under the words was a picture of a smiling couple, holding hands under a fiery tropic sun and gazing lovingly into each other's eyes.

Chase hadn't hesitated. He'd trotted across the street and straight into the travel agency. A bored clerk had looked up from a scarred wooden desk.

"We're just about to close," she'd said. "Why don't you come back tomorrow and—"

"That poster. The one in the window." He'd been too young, and too flushed with excitement, to phrase his question with any subtlety. "How much would it cost for me to take my wife to the Virgin Islands?"

The clerk had looked at the rose in his hand and the chocolates under his arm, and maybe at him, too, all youthful, eager anticipation, cleaned up but wearing, as he had in those years, the chambray shirt, jeans and work boots he felt most comfortable in. She'd sighed, but something that might have been a smile had lit her tired face.

"Come and sit down," she'd told him. "I have a couple of packages here that just might interest you."

So he'd gone home to Annie with one perfect red rose, a box of candy, a contract that made all his, and her, sacrifices worthwhile—and reservations at a resort on Saint John Island.

Neither the poster nor the travel agent had exaggerated the beauty of the islands. To this moment, he remembered the shock of first seeing the pale sky, white sand and crystal-clear blue water.

"It's the color of your eyes," he'd whispered to

Annie, as he held her in his arms that first night, in their wonderful hideaway overlooking the sea. Compared to this, the place had been a shack—but oh, how happy they'd been there!

Chase smiled to himself. That night had been what he'd come to think of as the Night of the Spider.

He and Annie had made love on the secluded terrace of their little house, cocooned in a black velvet bowl of night sky.

"I love you," he'd whispered, after she'd cried out in his arms and he'd spent himself in her silken heat. Annie had sighed and kissed him, and then they must have fallen asleep, there in the darkness with the soft whisper of the surf seeming to echo the beats of their hearts.

Sometime during the night, he'd awakened to a shriek.

"Annie?" he'd shouted, and though it had taken only a couple of seconds to race through the little house and find her in the bathroom, his adrenaline must have been pumping a mile a minute by the time he got there.

Annie, white-faced, was standing on the closed toilet, trembling with terror.

"Annie? Babe," he'd said, pulling her into his arms. "What is it? What happened?"

"There," she'd said, in a shaky whisper, and she'd pointed an equally shaky hand toward the tub.

"Where?" Chase had responded. All he saw was the porcelain tub, the bath mat, the gleaming white tile…

And the spider.

It was big, as spiders went. Definitely the large, economy size. And it was hairy. But it was only a spider, for God's sake, and in the time it had taken him to get from the bedroom to Annie, he'd died a thousand deaths, imagining what might have happened to her.

So he'd reacted the only way he could, scooping the

spider up with a towel, marching to the back door, dumping the thing into the sandy grass and then returning to his wife, slapping his hands on his hips and asking her what in hell was wrong with her, to shriek like a banshee because she saw some little spider that was probably more afraid of her than she was of it.

Annie had slapped her hands on her hips, too, and matched his angry glower with one of her own.

"That's it," she'd said, "take the spider's side instead of mine!"

"Are you nuts? I'm not taking—"

"You just think how you'd feel, if you'd come in here, turned on the light and found that—that thing waiting for you!"

"It wasn't 'waiting' for you. It was minding its own business."

"It was waiting for me," Annie had insisted, "tapping its eight trillion feet and waiting for—"

Chase had snorted. "Eight trillion feet?" he'd said, choking back his laughter, and suddenly Annie had started to laugh, too, and the next thing he'd known, his wife was in his arms.

"I know it's dumb," she'd said, laughing and crying at the same time, "but I'm scared of spiders. Especially big ones."

"Big?" Chase had said, cupping her face in his hands and smiling into her eyes. "Hey, that thing was big enough to eat Chicago." He'd stopped smiling then, and told her what was in his heart, that his anger had only been a cover-up for the fear he'd felt when he'd heard her scream, that if he ever lost her—that if he ever lost her, his life would have no meaning...

"Hi."

He swung around. Annie was standing in the doorway, smiling, and only force of will kept him from going to her, taking her in his arms, and telling her that—telling her that...

"Sorry I took so long, but I lost track of the time."

Chase expelled his breath and looked away from her.

"Were you gone long?" he said, with a casualness he didn't feel. "I hadn't noticed."

"I walked through the woods." Annie came closer, peered over his shoulder at the potatoes and onions and picked up a paring knife. "This is some beautiful place. I hate to think of it overrun with guys in three-piece suits."

Chase forced a smile to his lips. "They won't wear three-piece suits when they come here. They'll wear plaid Bermudas, black socks and wing tips."

Annie laughed, picked up a potato and began peeling it. "Same difference." They worked in silence for a few minutes, and then she spoke again. "I saw an interesting spider on the deck."

Chase looked up. "That's strange. I was just thinking about... Did you say, 'interesting'?"

"Uh-huh. It was..." She hesitated. "It was big. You know. Impressive."

"Impressive, huh? And you didn't scream? Seems to me I can remember the days when creepy crawlies weren't exactly your favorite creatures."

Annie blew an errant curl off her forehead. "They still aren't. But I took this course last year..."

"Why doesn't that surprise me?"

"It was about insects," she said with dignity.

That *did* surprise him. "You? Taking a course about bugs?"

Annie flushed. "Well, why not? I figured it was stupid to be scared of things with more than four legs. I decided, maybe if I understood them better, I might not jump at the sight of an ant."

"And?"

She shot him a sideways look and an embarrassed smile. "And, I learned to respect creepy crawlies like crazy. There are a heck of a lot more of them than there are of us, and they've been here longer."

Chase nodded. "I can almost hear the 'but' that's coming."

She laughed and reached for another potato. "But, I'm still not in the mood for a one-to-one relationship with anything that needs eight legs to cross a room."

Chase grinned. "It's nice to know that some things never change."

Annie's smile dimmed. "Yes. Yes, it is."

They worked in silence for a couple of minutes, Annie peeling potatoes, Chase slicing onions, and then Chase spoke.

"Annie?"

"Mmm?"

"I, ah, I wanted to tell you... I just hope you know..." He swallowed. "I didn't mean what I said before. About you taking all those courses to take digs at me, I mean."

Annie felt her cheeks redden. "That's okay."

"No. It's not okay. I know you enjoy learning all that stuff. The poetry, the art... It's just not my thing. Heck, if I'd had to take anything but the minimum liberal arts stuff to get my engineering degree, I'd never have managed. I'd probably still be digging ditches for a living."

Annie smiled and shook her head. "You know that's not true." She glanced at him, then put all her concentration on the potato she was peeling. "Anyway, maybe—maybe there was some truth to what you said. I mean, I didn't pick those things to study because I thought they'd, you know, be about stuff you wouldn't enjoy. I do like poetry, and art, and all the rest." She bent her head so that her hair fell around her face, shielding it from his view. "But I have to admit, when you looked puzzled about some eighteenth century poet, well, it made me feel good." She looked up suddenly, her eyes bright and shiny. "Not because I felt smarter or anything but because—because it was a way of proving that I could hold my own, you know? That even though I was only a housewife, that didn't mean I was—"

"*Only* a housewife?"

Annie shrugged as she dumped the potato on the counter and reached for another.

"That's what I was."

"Only a housewife," he said, and laughed. "That's a hell of a description for the woman who kept our home running smoothly, who raised our child, who entertained all the clowns I had to butter up while I was trying to get Cooper Construction moving."

"I guess I wasted an awful lot of time in self-pity."

"That's not what I meant. If anybody wasted time, babe, it was me. I should have told you how proud I was of all the things you did. But I was too busy patting myself on the back, congratulating myself for building Cooper Construction into something bigger than my father had ever dreamed. Something that would…"

Something that would make you proud of me, he'd almost said, but he stopped himself just in time. It was too late to talk about that now.

"Well, what's the difference?" he said briskly. "It's all water under the bridge." He concentrated on slicing the onions, and then he cleared his throat. "At least now I know that you didn't take all those classes just to get away from me."

"You weren't home often enough for me to worry about getting away from you," Annie said, a little stiffly.

"You could have had your degree by now," he said, wisely deciding it was the better part of valor to avoid a minefield than to attempt to cross it. "If you'd taken a concentration in one area, I mean."

"I don't need it." Annie peeled the last potato, put down her knife and wiped her hands on a towel. "All those horticulture courses paid off." A note of pride crept into her voice. "Flowers by Annie is a success, Chase. I've had to hire more people, and I'm thinking of maybe trying my hand at landscape design."

"That's wonderful."

"The truth is, I don't think I ever really wanted a degree. The thought of taking a bunch of formal classes didn't have any appeal. I just figured, well, I'd improve myself a little. Learn some stuff. You know."

"You didn't need improving," Chase said. He knew he sounded angry, but he couldn't help it. The only thing he didn't know was whether he was angry at Annie or himself. Improve herself? His Annie?

"I did. I just had this high school education..."

Chase dropped his paring knife, clasped her shoulders and turned her to face him.

"You were the valedictorian of your graduating class, dammit! The only reason you didn't go to college was because we got married, right after you graduated high school."

"I know. But—"

"We talked about it, remember? We tried to figure out if we could both go to college and still get married, and we decided we'd never be able to afford that." His mouth twisted. "So I went. You didn't. You took those miserable jobs, flipping hamburgers—"

"First, I flipped fish filets," Annie said with a shaky smile. "And then french fries. Hamburgers were a step up."

"Dammit, Annie, you gave up what you could have had, for me. Don't you think I know it?"

"I gave up nothing. I wanted to do it."

"Whatever we had—whatever I have, today—I owe to you."

"You don't owe me anything, Chase. You never did. Don't you understand?" Annie took a deep breath. "I didn't want a college degree half as much as I wanted to marry you."

"Yes." Chase's voice roughened. His hands slid up her throat and he buried them in her hair as he tilted her face to his. "That was all I could think of, too. Marrying you. Making you mine. So I did the selfish thing."

"You didn't!"

"I did, dammit!" His eyes searched her face, his gaze brushing her mouth before lifting again. "I let you give up your hopes and dreams so that I could have *my* dream."

"It was important to you. Becoming an engineer, making a success of yourself...."

"My dream was to have you. Only you. And, once I did, to give you the things you'd missed out on when we first got married, because you'd had to make so many sacrifices."

"They weren't sacrifices," Annie said, as the tears rose in her eyes. "I loved you, Chase. I wanted to help you succeed."

"And I only wanted to make you proud of me."

They fell silent.

If only I'd known, Annie thought...

If only I'd understood, Chase thought...

Was it too late? he wondered. Could you turn back the years? Could that be something this beautiful, confident woman in his arms might even want to do? She'd turned into someone else, his Annie, a stranger with a life of her own.

Was it too late? Annie wondered. Was it possible to roll back time? They were two different people now, she and this handsome, wonderful man who had once been her husband. He had moved into a high-powered world that was eons removed from her quiet country life.

And then, there was Janet Pendleton. The woman Chase was engaged to marry. The woman he loved.

Tears stung Annie's eyes. What an idiot she was! How could she have forgotten? They'd moved on, the both of them, and Chase had found someone to replace her, in his heart and in his life.

She swallowed hard. Chase was looking at her so strangely. Oh, how tempting it was to let herself believe, just for an instant, for a heartbeat, that he still loved her. But she knew that he didn't. What she saw in his eyes was regret for the pain they'd caused each other, and compassion—but not love.

Not anymore.

"Annie." His voice was soft, almost tender. "Annie," he said, "I'm so sorry."

"Don't be," she said quickly. Compassion was one thing, but pity was another. Pity was the last thing she wanted from Chase. "There's no point. It's spilt milk, you know?" It wasn't easy, but she smiled. "And nobody should ever waste tears over spilt milk."

"It's not that simple."

"But it is." Annie spoke quickly, rushing her words, hurrying to keep him from offering her another apology. What she wanted from him, needed with all her heart, was something she wouldn't think about, wouldn't admit to thinking about, even to herself. "It's very simple," she said, with another little smile. "It looks as if us spending time together was a good idea, after all."

"Yes. I agree."

"If we hadn't, we'd never have gotten this chance to—to make peace with the past."

"Can you forgive me, for hurting you?"

"Of course." It was easier to smile, now that she knew it was the only choice left to her. "As long as you can forgive me, too, because I wasn't blameless. And then, we get on with our lives. With—with our new relationships."

The tiny flame of hope in Chase's heart flickered and died.

"Milton Hoffman." His voice was toneless.

"And your Janet Pendleton. Yes."

Chase could see the radiance in Annie's smile. It lit her eyes. Funny, but a couple of minutes ago, he'd foolishly let himself think the light in her eyes was for him.

"We're very fortunate people," she said softly. "Some never find love once but we—we found it twice."

Chase stared at the stranger who had once been his wife. He thought of pulling her into his embrace and kissing her until that smile for Milton Hoffman was erased from her lips. He thought of kissing her until all she could think of was him.

But, in the end, he did what he knew was right.

"That's true," he said, touching his hand to her hair, because he couldn't keep from doing it. He kept the touch light, though, so that it matched his smile. "We're very lucky, the both of us."

He let go of her, turned away and reached blindly for a peeled onion. Annie watched, her heart breaking, as he sliced into it. She felt the sting of tears again and she scrubbed the back of her hand furiously over her eyes.

"Damned onions," she said, with a choked laugh. "You're slicing them but I'm suffering. Isn't that silly?"

Chase, lost in his own thoughts, nodded. "Yeah."

"So," she said briskly, "what are we having for supper, anyway? Onion and potato pie?"

Somehow, he forced his attention back to the kitchen, and the mundane chores they were performing. He smiled, put down the knife, wiped his hands on the towel and opened the door of the cabinet just over the sink.

"*Voilà*," he said, whipping around to face Annie and holding out a small, round can as if he were a sommelier presenting her with a bottle of fine wine.

"Tuna? That's it? That's all you could find in this kitchen?"

"There's another half a dozen, right on the pantry shelf."

"I don't believe it. All this, and Mr. Tanaka eats canned tuna?"

"I don't think sushi would have much of a shelf life." Chase grinned. "Less than thrilling, huh?"

"You're sure there isn't anything else?"

"A couple of cans of evaporated milk. A bottle of corn oil. Some soup—"

"Cream of mushroom?" she asked hopefully.

"Yeah. I think so."

Annie sighed. "Get me the soup and the evaporated milk, Cooper. Then step aside and let an expert get to work."

"You mean, you can do something clever with this stuff?"

"I can try."

Chase grinned as he plucked the other cans from the shelves, opened them and put them on the counter.

"I should have known. I'd almost forgotten how inventive you were with Spam, the first couple of years after we were married."

"Inventive?" Annie said, as she drained the tuna into the sink.

"Sure. Seems to me I can remember Spam casserole, sautéed Spam, grilled Spam…"

"A can of Spam, a couple of onions and some potatoes."

"Which recipe was that?"

"All of them," Annie said, laughing. She dug around in the shelves beneath the stove, took out a skillet and put it on a burner. "I kept giving the same concoction different names, to keep us from going whacko."

"Now she tells me. So, what's on the menu tonight?"

"How about Tuna Surprise?"

"What's the Surprise?"

"Managing to turn this mess into something edible," Annie said, and laughed. "Here. Start dicing the potatoes. I'll heat up some oil and slice the rest of the onions."

"Suppose you supervise while I do the work. It's my fault we're stuck out here, in the tail end of nowhere, so it's only fair I get to make dinner."

"Let's face it, Cooper. We're trapped in a place most people would kill for, so stop apologizing and start dicing."

Annie splashed some oil into the skillet, then leaned past Chase and placed it on the burner. Her breast brushed lightly across his arm, and he felt himself harden like stone. Desire, an overpowering need for her, for Annie, the mother of his child and the passion of his youth, surged through his blood, pumping hard and hot, and pooled low in his belly.

He jerked away. As he did, his elbow knocked against the knife and it clattered to the floor.

"Damn," he said, as if it mattered, as if anything mattered but wanting to take his wife in his arms.

Milton Hoffman's face, the face of the man she loved, rose before him as if it were an apparition. Hoffman, who couldn't love Annie as much as he did because, dammit, he *did* love her. Not again, but still. He'd never stopped loving her, and it was time to admit it.

"Annie," he said in a low voice.

Annie looked up. The temperature in the kitchen felt as if it had gone up ten degrees.

The message was there, in Chase's eyes. Her heart leaped in her chest. She told herself not to be a fool. What was happening here wasn't real. Reality was the papers that had legally severed their marriage. It was a woman named Janet, waiting for Chase back in New York.

On the other hand, hadn't some philosopher said reality was what you made of it?

"Annie?" Chase whispered. He reached toward her and she swayed forward, her eyes half-closed...

The smell of burning oil filled the kitchen.

Annie swung around, grabbed the skillet and dumped it into the sink.

"We'll have to start over," she said, with a shaky laugh. She looked at Chase. "With the cooking, I mean."

Chase nodded. Then they turned away from each other and made a show of being busy.

Annie fried more onions, parboiled the diced potatoes and put together a tuna casserole.

Chase made the coffee and opened a package of crackers and a box of cookies.

When everything was ready, they carried their meal into the living room, arranged it on the low, lacquered table and sat, cross-legged, on the black-and-white cushions. They ate in silence, as politely and impersonally as if they were strangers who'd been asked to share a table in a crowded coffee shop.

Afterward, they cleaned up together. Then Annie took a magazine from a stack she'd found in the kitchen.

Chase said he'd take another walk.

Annie said she'd read.

But she didn't. The black-and-white cushions didn't offer much in the way of comfort. Besides, her thoughts kept straying away from the magazine, to the hours looming ahead. There was an entire night to get through. She and Chase, sharing this cabin. And that bedroom.

How would she manage?

She jumped when Chase stepped into the living room.

"Sorry," he said. "I didn't meant to startle you."

"That's okay." She folded her hands over the closed magazine, her fingers knotted tightly together. "I was thinking," she said carefully. "I mean, it occurred to me..."

"What?"

Annie took a breath.

"Well, there is one advantage to being here by ourselves."

Chase looked at her. His eyes were burning like coals. "There's a definite advantage."

There was no mistaking his meaning. Annie felt her heart swell, as if it were a balloon, until it seemed to fill her chest.

"What I mean," she said, speaking with care, "is that there's no one here to know what our arrangements are. We wouldn't have to explain anything..." Her words stuttered to a halt. "Don't look at me that way," she whispered.

Chase shut the door, his eyes locked on hers. "Do you want to make love?"

The directness of the question stole her breath away. She shook her head. "No! I didn't say—"

"I want you, Annie."

His voice was rough and his face seemed to have taken on an angularity, but she knew what she was really seeing was desire. She knew, because this was how he'd looked, years ago, when their need for each other had been an unquenchable thirst. They'd be talking, or just sitting and reading or watching TV, and suddenly she'd feel a stillness in the air. And she'd look up, and Chase would be watching her, and what she saw in his eyes would make her breasts swell so that she'd feel the scrape of her bra against her nipples, feel the dampness bloom between her thighs...

"Babe," he said thickly, "I want you so much I can't think straight."

It seemed to take forever before she could draw enough strength to answer.

"We can't," she said, in a voice that sounded like a stranger's.

"Why? We're adults. Who is it going to hurt, if we do what we both want to do?"

Me, she'd thought, me, Chase, because if I go to bed with you, I'll be forced to admit the truth to myself, that I still—that I still—

"No," she said, her voice rising in a cry that seemed to tremble in the air between them. "No," she repeated, and then, because it was the only safe thing she could think of, she took another breath and lied again, the same way she had when they'd been preparing dinner. "It wouldn't be fair to—to Milton."

"Milton." The name was like an obscenity on Chase's lips.

"That's right. Milton. I'm engaged, and so are you. What I meant about nobody knowing what we do tonight, nobody asking questions, was that there's no reason for us to share the bedroom.''

''I see.''

She waited for him to say something else, but he didn't.

''Surely, in this entire house, there's another—''

''No.''

''No?''

''Look around you, dammit. There's no sofa. There's not even a chair, except for the rocker in the bedroom.''

Annie stared at him, wondering why he sounded so angry.

''Well,'' she said, looking up at the ceiling, ''what's on the second—''

''Did you see a staircase?''

''Well—well, no. No, I didn't. But—''

''That's because there aren't any rooms above us. There's just a storage loft, full of boxes. And bats.''

''Bats?'' Annie said, with a faint shudder.

''Bats,'' Chase repeated coldly, furious at her, at himself, at Dawn, at Kichiro Tanaka and the city of Seattle and the Fates and whoever, whatever, had put him into this impossible situation. His lips drew back from his teeth. ''The bats eat the spiders. The *impressive* ones, the size of dinner plates.''

''In other words, you're telling me we'll have to make the best of things.''

''A brilliant deduction.''

Annie tossed aside the magazine and shot to her feet. ''Listen, Cooper, don't be so high-and-mighty! I'm not the one who got us stuck out here, and don't you forget it.''

''No,'' he snarled, ''I won't forget it. If you'd put your foot down in the first place, if you'd told our daughter, flat out, that she couldn't marry Nick—''

"That's it," Annie said, stalking past him.

"Don't you walk out on me, lady."

"I'm going to find something else to read," she snapped, over her shoulder. "Even the label on a can of tuna would be better than trying to have a conversation with you."

"You're right," Chase snapped back, shouldering past her. "I might even take my chances and try swimming to the mainland. Anything would be an improvement over an evening spent in your company!"

Annie sat on the rocker in the bedroom. She looked at her watch.

Chase had been gone a long time. Surely he hadn't really meant that. He wouldn't have really tried to swim the cold, choppy water...

The bedroom door opened. She looked up and saw Chase.

"Sorry," he said briskly. "I should have knocked."

"That's all right. I, uh, I was just sitting here and—and thinking."

"It's been a long day. I don't know about you, but I'd just as soon turn in and get some sleep."

"That's what I was thinking about. Our sleeping arrangements. We can share the room."

"We *are* sharing it," he said coldly. "I thought I'd made that clear. There isn't a hell of a lot of choice."

"You did. And I—I agree. It's not a problem," Annie said, rushing her words together. "The bed's the size of a football field. I'll take the right side. You can have... What are you doing?"

Chase was yanking open closet doors. "There've got to be linens here somewhere... Here we go." He reached inside, took out an armful of bedding, tossed a blanket to Annie and then draped another over the rocker.

"You're going to sleep in the chair?"

"That's right." He sat down, tucked a pillow behind his head and stretched out his legs. "I wouldn't want to sully your reputation."

"Chase, please. I never meant—"

He reached behind him, hit the switch on the wall and the room was plunged into darkness. Annie closed her eyes. Tears seeped out from beneath her lashes.

"Chase?" she whispered, after a long time.

"What?"

"Nothing," she said, and rolled onto her side.

I love you, Chase, she thought, because there was no harm in saying it now, to herself, even as she wondered how she was going to get through the endless night.

"Good night, Annie," Chase said, and he shifted uneasily, trying to find a comfortable position even though he knew there was no such thing, not in a wooden rocker, not with the granddaddy of all headaches in permanent residence behind his temples—and not with the only woman he would ever love sleeping a hand's span away.

He could smell her perfumed scent, hear the softness of her breathing. All he had to do was reach out and he'd be able to touch her warm, silken skin.

How in hell was he ever going to get through the night?

CHAPTER NINE

CHASE CAME AWAKE with a start. The room was inky black; he could hear the light patter of rain against the roof.

Where was he? Not at home, that was for sure.

Memory came back in a rush. The crazy flight to Seattle. The motorboat, speeding across the water. The island. The cabin. The bedroom…

This bedroom.

And Annie. Annie, asleep in a bed inches from where he sat.

Don't think about that. About Annie. Think about something else. Anything else.

Chase grimaced. He could think about how it would be a miracle if he ever managed to stand upright again. Now, that was a topic worth considering.

Gingerly, hands clasping the arms of the wooden rocker, he eased himself up so that his back was straight. Not that caution would make much difference. His spine felt as brittle as china, and it ached like hell. The rest of him didn't feel much better.

Whistler's Mother be damned, he thought grimly. Wooden rocking chairs were not made for comfort, or for sleeping.

It was chilly in here, too. It didn't help that the blanket he'd draped over himself was somewhere on the floor. Wincing, he bent down and felt around until he found it. Then he dragged it up to his neck and told himself that this night couldn't last forever.

What time was it, anyway? Chase raised his arm and

peered at the place on his wrist where he knew his watch ought to be. The lighted dial was faint; he had to squint to see it clearly. It had to be, what? Three, maybe four in the morning?

Bloody hell! It was eleven twenty-five. He'd been asleep, if you could call it that, all of two hours.

Wearily he closed his eyes, started to put his head back and remembered, just in time, that if he did, he'd whack his skull against the wall. He'd done it a couple of times already. For all he knew, that was what had awakened him in the first place.

Eleven twenty-five. Unbelievable! If he were in Seattle right now, he'd be wide-awake. He'd be sitting up in a nice, soft bed, with a pillow tucked between him and the headboard, and he'd be reading. Or watching TV. Making notes for the next day's meetings. Whatever. The one sure thing was that he wouldn't be sitting in the most uncomfortable chair man had ever invented, with no place to rest his head. Or his legs. As for his butt...men, he'd decided, were not born with enough padding where it counted.

Another couple of hours, he'd end up a chiropractor's dream.

Dammit, who was he kidding? Another couple of minutes, he'd end up out of his skull. Forget the chair, and the discomfort of trying to sleep in it. Forget the night chill that had seeped into the room. Forget the soft whisper of the rain.

None of that was the reason he was awake.

The reason, plain and simple, was Annie.

How was he supposed to get through the night trapped in this room with her?

Chase told himself he ought to be ashamed for his lecherous thoughts. Not that they were his fault. It was Annie who was to blame.

Damn. Oh damn. Why couldn't he admit the truth? There was no way to lay this off on Annie. She hadn't planted these pictures in his head. She couldn't possibly know he was sitting here with an aching back and a sizzling libido. She was sound asleep. He could tell by the soft, steady whisper of her breath. If he'd been having raunchy dreams—and he had—it was nobody's fault but his own.

One dream, in particular, had been very real.

It had started with him sitting right here, in this chair, when he'd heard Annie sigh his name.

Chase, she'd said, and suddenly moonlight had streamed into the room, casting an ivory glow on the bed.

Annie had sat up and opened her arms to him.

Chase, she'd whispered, *why are you sitting over there? Come to bed, darling, with me, where you belong.*

Chase rubbed his hands over his eyes.

"Give us a break, Cooper," he muttered. "What are you, a pimply-faced kid?"

A grown man could share a room with a woman for the night without coming unglued, especially when she was the very woman he'd divorced five long years ago. He could get through twenty-four hours without letting himself think he'd fallen for her all over again because the truth was, he hadn't.

Of course he hadn't.

It was just the pressure of the last few days, that was all. Things were catching up. The wedding. Dawn's running away. His emotional and physical exhaustion. Taken all together, it was a prescription for disaster.

Then, too, his ex was still a very attractive woman. His type of woman, which was only logical considering that he'd been married to her, once upon a time. But he'd also left her, or they'd left each other, to be exact, and for very good reasons.

Chase sat back carefully in the rocker.

So, okay, she could still push all the right buttons. And yeah, his stupid male hormones were still programmed to make his equally stupid male anatomy straighten up and salute. That didn't mean he had to sit here having thoughts that were beginning to make going out into the rain for an impromptu shower seem like a pretty good idea.

He had to concentrate on the reality of the situation. Annie was in love with another man, and if he wasn't actually feeling the same way about Janet, well, he could. He would. It was just a matter of letting it happen. And then the story of Annie and Chase would be over, once and for all.

Dawn was a big girl now. She'd understand that life wasn't a fairy tale that ended with the words, "And they lived happily ever after."

Chase sighed. He felt better already. There'd be no more dreams tonight. Why, even if that last silly dream were to come true, if Annie were to suddenly stir and whisper his name, he wouldn't—

"Chase?"

Annie's voice, as soft and sweet as an early June morning, turned that firm conviction into an instant lie.

"Chase? Are you awake?"

Was he awake? He couldn't imagine why she had to ask. Couldn't she hear the thunder of his heart?

He heard the rustle of the bed linens as she turned toward him. Her face was a pale, perfect oval; her eyes were wide and gleaming. Her hair curled around her face and neck, falling in a gentle curve to her shoulder.

How he'd always loved to kiss her there, in the satin-softness of that curve.

Chase cleared his throat. "Hi," he said. "Sorry if I woke you."

Annie shook her head. "You didn't. Not really. I had a silly dream—"

She broke off in the middle of what she'd been about to say, grateful for the lack of light in the room because it meant Chase couldn't see the blush she knew was spreading over her face. It was bad enough she'd had the dream in the first place. She certainly wasn't going to describe it to him.

Why would any woman in her right mind tell her ex-husband about an erotic dream—especially when she, and he, had been its stars?

"What dream?"

"I don't remember."

"But you just said—"

"What's that I hear? Rain?"

Annie sat up against the pillows and drew the blanket up to her chin. Her arms and shoulders were bare. Chase's heart lifted into his throat. Was she naked under that blanket?

"Yes," he said in a voice that sounded more like a croak but hey, a man had to be happy for what he could manage and right now, managing even that much was a miracle.

Annie sighed. "Mmm. It sounds wonderful, doesn't it? It makes it seem so cozy in here."

Cozy? Chase almost groaned. "Yeah," he said, "oh, yeah, cozy's the word."

"What time is it, anyway? Is it close to morning? I could make us some coffee."

"It's almost twelve."

"Twelve? How could that be? It's so dark..." Annie gave an incredulous laugh. "Twelve at *night*? You're joking."

"I wish I were."

Annie's head drooped. There was still an entire night, stretching ahead. Hours and hours of lying here, knowing she had only to reach out her hand to touch the man who'd once been her husband.

No. This was impossible. She could never survive until morning…

Of course she could. She wasn't foolish enough to still think herself in love with Chase. That nonsense had faded away while she'd slept. What she felt was lust, pure and simple. Hey, she could admit it. This was the end of one century and the start of another. Women were allowed to have sexual feelings. They were encouraged to have them, according to the talk shows on TV and the supermarket tabloids.

And she had them. Oh, yes, she did. Chase had always been—probably always would be—the kind of man who could turn her on with a look, but wanting sex with a man didn't necessarily have anything to do with loving him, despite what she'd told Chase when they'd talked about Dawn and Nick, just yesterday.

The truth was, sex was all a matter of hormones and libido. Love was a separate thing entirely. Everybody said so, even Milton, who'd earnestly assured her that it was okay if she didn't feel anything for him physically. They could still have a good life together, he'd said.

Maybe he was right.

"Annie?"

She blinked and lifted her head. Her eyes had grown accustomed to the lack of light in the bedroom. She could see Chase clearly now, sitting in the rocker and watching her.

"What are you thinking?"

"Nothing," she said quickly, "only that—that it's

amazing if Mr. Tanaka ever manages to get any sleep in this bed. The mattress feels as if it's stuffed with steel."

Chase laughed. "Welcome to the Chamber of Horrors. Did President Kennedy really sit in one of these godawful chairs to ease the pain in his back?"

"I don't think he tried to substitute a rocker for a bed," Annie said, smiling.

"Well, that's why he got to be president. The guy was smart."

Annie laughed. It was such a light, easy sound that it made Chase smile. There was a time they'd laughed a lot together. Not over anything special. Just something one would see or hear and say to the other, or something that would happen when they were together.

It felt good, making her laugh again. Everything about today had felt good, even the moments they'd been going at each other. An argument with Annie was better than an evening of smiles from any other woman, especially if the argument ended, as it so often had, in the old days, with her in his arms...in his arms, and wanting him as much as he wanted her.

What would she do, if he went to her now? If he shucked off his clothes, pulled back the blankets and got into the bed with her? He knew just how she would smell, like a blend of perfume and honey and cream. And how she would feel, the heat of her breasts and belly, the coolness of her hands and feet.

He smiled, remembering. Lord, she had the iciest hands and feet in the world!

It was a game they'd often played, on chilly nights like this. They'd get into bed, he'd take her in his arms and she'd wrap one leg around his, dance her toes over his calf while she slid her hand down his chest and he'd say, very sternly, Annie, you stop that right now, and she'd ask why and he'd say because she was positively frigid.

"Frigid?" she'd say, indignantly.

"Frigid," he'd insist, and then he'd roll her onto her back and whisper, "but I know a way to fix that…"

Chase shot to his feet.

"Here," he said gruffly, dumping the blanket he'd been using on Annie's bed. "Take this. It's gotten a little chilly in here."

"I'm fine. Anyway, I can't take your blanket."

"Sure you can."

"But what'll you use?"

A snowbank, if he could find one. What he needed was not to warm up but to chill down.

"I'm, ah, I'm not tired."

"Not tired? Chase, that's impossible. We've had an awful day. An endless day—"

"You've got that right."

"And you've only had, what, two hours sleep? That's not enough."

"Yeah, well, maybe I'm overwound. Or maybe it's just that I'm not in the mood to turn into a human pretzel."

"You're right." Annie reached for his discarded blanket. In one quick motion, she dropped her own blanket, wrapped his around her shoulders, and rose from the bed. Chase had a glimpse of ivory-colored skin and nothing more. "So you take the bed. I'll take the chair."

"Don't be ridiculous."

"I'm smaller than you are."

She was. Definitely. Smaller, and fragile. Wonderfully fragile. Make that feminine. The top of her head barely brushed his chin. If he dipped his head, he could rub his chin against her hair. Her soft, shiny hair.

"I can tuck my legs up under me and I'll be perfectly

comfortable, Chase. You'll see. Come on. Switch places with me.''

Switch places? Climb into the bed, still warm from her body? Put his head on the pillow, still fragrant with her scent? He shook his head and moved back, until the seat of the rocker dug into the backs of his legs.

''No.''

''Honestly, you're such a chauvinist! This is hardly a time to worry about being a gentleman.''

He had to fight hard to keep from laughing. Or groaning. One or the other, or maybe both. Is that what she thought this was all about? Him trying to be a gentleman? He wondered what she'd think if she knew the real direction of his thoughts, that it was all he could do to keep from picking her up, tossing her onto the bed and tearing away that blanket so he could see if she was wearing anything under it.

''That's it,'' he said.

''What's it?''

Chase cupped Annie's shoulders, trying not to think about the feel of her under his hands, and moved her gently but firmly out of his way.

''Chase?'' Her voice rang with bewilderment as he opened the door. ''Where are you going?''

To hell in a handbasket, he thought.

''To heat up some coffee,'' he said. ''Go back to sleep, Annie. I'll see you in the morning.''

He slipped out of the room, shut the door after him and leaned back against it.

The torture of the chair was one thing. A man could deal with that. But the torture of being so close to Annie was something else.

Saints willingly martyred themselves, not men.

* * *

Annie stared at the door as it swung shut. Then she sighed and sank down on the edge of the bed.

"Stupid man," she muttered. "Let him suffer, if he wants."

It was ridiculous of him to have turned down her offer.

"Brrr," she said, and burrowed under the covers.

Of course, he'd been uncomfortable in that chair. Chase was six foot two; he'd weighed 190 pounds for as long as she could remember, all of it muscle. Hard muscle.

There was no denying that he'd always been a handsome man.

Beautiful, she'd called him once, after they were first married. They'd been lying in each other's arms after a long, lazy afternoon of love, and suddenly she'd risen up on her elbows, gazed down at him and smiled.

"What?" he'd said, and she'd said she'd never thought about it before, but he was beautiful.

"Goofball," Chase had said, laughing. "Men can't be 'beautiful.'"

"Why can't they?" she'd said, in a perfectly reasonable tone, and then, in that same tone, she'd gone on to list all his attributes, and to kiss them all, too. His nose. His mouth. His chin. His broad shoulders. His lightly furred chest. His flat abdomen and belly...

"Annie," he'd said, in a choked whisper, and seconds later he'd hauled her up his body, into his arms and taken her into the star-shot darkness with him again.

"Dammit!"

Annie flung out her arms and stared up at the skylight, where the light rain danced gently against the glass. What was wrong with her tonight? First the dream that had left her aching and unfulfilled. And now this ridiculous, pointless memory.

"You're being a ninny," she said out loud.

She wasn't in love with Chase; hadn't she already admitted that? As for the sex... Okay. So sex with him had always been good.

Until he'd ruined it, by never coming home to her.

Until she'd ruined it, by treating him so coldly.

Annie threw her arm across her eyes.

All right. So she wasn't as blameless as she liked to think. But Chase had hurt her so badly. Nothing had prepared her for the pain of watching him grow out of her life, or of finding him with his secretary...

Or for the pain of losing him.

The truth was that she'd never stopped wanting him. Her throat tightened. Never. Not then. Not all the years since. If he'd taken her in his arms again tonight, if he'd kissed her, stroked his hand over her skin...

The door banged open. Annie grabbed for the blanket and sat up, clutching it to her chin. Chase stood framed in the doorway. Light streamed down the hall, illuminating his face and body with shimmering rays of gold.

"Annie."

His voice was soft and husky. The sound of it sent her heartbeat racing. Say something, she told herself, but her throat felt paralyzed.

"Annie." He stepped into the room, his eyes locked on hers. "I lied," he said. "It isn't the chair that kept me from sleeping. It's you."

It was a moment for a flippant remark. A little humor, a little sarcasm; something along the lines of, "Really? Well, it's good to know I'm giving you a bad time."

But she didn't want to toss him a fast one-liner.

She wanted what he wanted. Why keep up the pretense any longer?

They were two adults, alone on an island that might just as easily have been spinning in the dark reaches of space instead of being just off the Washington coast. Going into Chase's arms, loving him just for tonight, would hurt no one.

He has a fiancée, a voice inside her whispered. *He belongs to another woman now.*

"Annie? I want to make love to you. I *need* to make love to you. Tell me to go away, babe, and I will, if that's what you really want, but I don't think it is. I think you want to come into my arms and taste my kisses. I think you want us to hold each other, the way we used to."

The blanket fell from Annie's hands. She gave a little sob and her arms opened wide.

Chase whispered her name, pulled off his clothes and went to her.

He kissed her mouth, and her throat. He kissed the soft skin behind her ear and buried his face in that sweet curve of neck and shoulder that felt like warm silk.

She'd been wearing something under the blanket, after all. A bra and panties, just plain white cotton, but he thought he'd never seen anything as sexy in his life. His hands had never trembled more than they did as he unfastened the bra and slid the panties down Annie's long legs.

"My beautiful Annie," he murmured, when she lay naked in his arms.

"I'm not," she said, with a little catch in her throat. "I'm older. Everything's starting to sag."

Her breath caught as Chase bent and kissed the slope of her breast.

"You're perfect," he whispered, his breath warm against her flesh. "More beautiful than before."

His hands cupped her breasts; he bent his head and licked her nipples. It was the truth. She'd gone from being a lovely girl to being a beautiful woman. Her body was classic in its femininity, lushly curved and warm with desire beneath his hands and his mouth. Annie smelled like rosebuds and warm honey, and she tasted like the nectar of the gods.

She was a feast for a man who'd been starving for five long, lonely years.

"Chase," she whispered, when he kissed his way down her belly. Her voice broke as he parted her thighs. "Chase," she said again.

He looked up at her, his eyes dark and fierce. "I never forgot," he said. "The smell of you. The heat." His hands clasped her thighs. Slowly he lowered his head. "The taste."

Annie cried out as his mouth found her. It had been so long. Five years of lonely nights and empty days, of wanting Chase and never admitting it, of dreaming of him, of this, and then denying the dreams in the morning.

I love you, she thought fiercely, Chase, my husband, my beloved, I adore you. How could I have ever forgotten that?

He kissed her again and she shattered against the kiss, tumbling through the darkness of the night, and just before she fell to earth he rose up over her and thrust into her body with one deep, hard stroke.

"Chase," she cried, and this time, when she came, he was with her, holding her tightly in his arms as they made the breathless free fall through space together.

The last thing she saw, just before she fell asleep in his arms, was the crescent moon, framed overhead in the skylight, as the clouds parted and the gentle rain ceased.

She awakened during the night, to the soft brush of Chase's mouth against her nape.

It was as if the years had fallen away. How many

times had she come awake to his kisses, and to his touch?

"I never stopped thinking about you," he whispered.

I never stopped loving you, was what he wanted to say, but he wanted to look into her eyes when he did, to read her answer there.

So he spoke to her with his body instead, burying himself in her heat, one hand on her breast and the other low across her belly, moving within her, matching his rhythm to hers, until he groaned and she cried out. Then he turned her into his embrace, kissed her and slipped inside her again, still hard, still wanting her, and this time when she came, she wept.

"Did I hurt you?" he said softly, and for an instant she almost told him that the pain would come in the morning, when the sun rose and the night ended, and all of this would be nothing more substantial than a dream.

But that would be wrong. This *was* a dream, and she knew it. So she smiled against his mouth and said no, he hadn't hurt her, and then she sighed and put her head on his shoulder.

"Annie?"

"Mmm?"

"I've been thinking." He kissed her, and she could feel the smile on his lips. "We ought to try out that tub."

"Mmm," she said again. She yawned lazily. "First thing in the morning…"

And she drifted off to sleep.

Sunlight woke them—sunlight, and the hornet buzz of the motorboat.

Annie jumped up in bed, heart pounding.

"What…?"

Chase was already pulling on his chinos and zipping up his fly.

"It's okay, babe," he said. "I'll take care of things."

She nodded, put her hands to her face and pushed back her hair. Chase started for the door, hesitated, and came back.

"Annie," he said, and when she looked up, he bent to her and kissed her. "It was a wonderful night," he said softly.

She nodded. "Yes. It was."

For a minute, she thought he was going to say something more but then he turned away and snagged his shirt from the chair just as a knock sounded at the front door.

"Okay, okay," he yelled, "hold your horses. I'm coming." He swung back one last time, just before he opened the door. "Wonderful," he said. "And I'm never going to forget it."

Annie smiled, even though she could feel tears stinging her eyes.

Chase's message had been gallant, to the point and painfully clear.

It had been a wonderful night. But it was morning now, and what they'd shared was over.

CHAPTER TEN

ANNIE STARTED DOWN the steps of her sister's apartment building just as the skies opened up.

It had been raining, on and off, for most of the sultry August afternoon but half an hour ago the sky had cleared and so the cloudburst took her by surprise. She gave a startled yelp and darted back into the vestibule of the converted brownstone.

Wonderful, she thought, as fat raindrops pounded the hot pavement. Just what she needed. A steamy day, and now a hard rain. By the time she got to the subway entrance, she'd be not only drenched but boiled.

Annie looked over her shoulder. Should she ring the intercom bell? She could ask Laurel to buzz her in, go back upstairs and keep her sister company a while longer.

No, she thought, and sighed. That wouldn't be such a good idea. Laurel might have fallen asleep by now. She'd promised she was going to lie down and take a nap, right after Annie left. Heaven knew she looked as if she needed the rest.

Laurel was going through a bad time.

Hell. A bad time was putting it mildly.

Annie hadn't wanted to leave her, not even when it began to get late and it looked as if she might miss the last train for Stratham.

"You're sure you're okay?" she'd said to Laurel.

"I'm fine," Laurel had replied.

The sisters both knew it was a lie.

Laurel was not fine. She was pregnant and alone and

161

desperately in love with a husband who'd maybe two-timed her or maybe hadn't, depending on whose story you believed. Either way, it broke Annie's heart to see her little sister looking so beautiful and feeling so sad.

"Men," Annie muttered with disgust.

Not a one of them was worth a penny. Well, her son-in-law was an exception. Annie's features softened. Nick was a sweetheart. But the rest of the male species was impossible.

She blew her curls away from her forehead. The vestibule was turning into a sauna. She'd have to make a run for it soon, even though she could still hear the rain beating down as if the heavenly floodgates had opened and Noah was giving the last call for the Ark.

Boy, it was really coming down. People always said it rained hard in the Pacific northwest, but the night she'd been there, the rain had been as soft as a lover's caress.

Annie frowned. What nonsense! She hadn't wasted a minute thinking about that awful night, and now it had popped into her head, wrapped in a bit of purple prose that would make any levelheaded female retch.

It was the rain that had done it. And spending the day with Laurel. What was the matter with the two of them? Were the Bennett sisters doomed to go through life behaving like idiots?

No way. Laurel would pull herself together, the same as she'd always done. As for her... Annie straightened her shoulders. She was not going to think about that night, or Chase. Why would she? She wasn't a masochist, and only a masochist would want to remember making a fool of herself, because that was what she'd done on that island.

Falling for her ex's lying, sexy charm, tumbling into his arms, inviting him into her bed and making it embarrassingly clear that she'd enjoyed having him there…so clear that he'd figured she'd be only too happy to offer a repeat performance.

Chase had phoned with that in mind several times since.

She'd talked with him the first time, because she knew they'd had to agree on what to tell Dawn when she and Nick returned from Hawaii.

"What do you want to tell her?" Chase had asked, neatly dumping the problem into her lap.

"The truth," Annie had answered, "that you lied and I was dumb enough to go along with it—but that would probably be a mistake. So why don't we settle for something simple. Like, we spent the weekend together and it just didn't work out."

"We didn't spend the weekend together," Chase had said. "It was only one night. But it doesn't have to end there."

Apparently behaving like an idiot once didn't keep you from behaving like one all over again. Annie's heart had done those silly flip-flops that she hated and she'd waited, barely breathing, for him to say he loved her.

But he hadn't.

"I know you don't want to get involved again," he'd said in the same, reasonable tone a TV pitchman might have used selling used cars, "but you have to admit, that night was—it was memorable."

"Memorable," Annie had repeated calmly.

"Yes. And I'd like to see you again."

She could still remember how she'd felt, the pain and the rage twisting inside her so she hadn't been sure which she wanted to do first, cry her eyes out or kill him.

"I'll just bet you would," she'd said, with dignity, and then she'd hung up the phone, poured herself a double sherry and toasted the brilliance she'd shown on having removed Mr. Chase Cooper from her life five long years ago.

At least he'd been up-front about what he wanted. And talkative, especially compared to the silent act he'd put on that morning on the island. He hadn't said more than half a dozen words to her, after the guy had come to fetch them with the motorboat.

Not that she'd given him the chance to say much of anything. She'd done something foolish by sleeping with Chase but she wasn't stupid: that remark about what a wonderful night it had been wasn't anything but code for "Thanks for the roll in the hay, babe," and she knew it. The quick brush-off had almost broken her heart, but she'd sooner have died than let Chase know it. So she'd put on what she'd figured was a look of morning-after sophistication, as if one-night stands were part of her life, and ignored him until they reached the airport, where she'd smiled brightly, shaken his hand and said it had been a delightful evening and she hoped his meeting with Mr. Tanaka went well.

Then she'd marched off, bought herself a ticket back to Connecticut, and done her weeping alone in the back of a nearly empty jet throughout the long flight home.

Sex, that was all Chase had wanted. But that was okay. Sex was all she'd wanted from him, too. She understood that now. Five years was a long time for a healthy woman to go without a man. And, she thought coldly, Chase was good in bed. It was just too bad that even in this era of female liberation, she'd had to delude herself into thinking she loved him before she could sleep with him.

Well, it wouldn't happen again, despite his eager hopes for a repeat performance. Let him wrestle between the sheets with his fiancée—not that being engaged had stopped him that night. Why would it? Fidelity wasn't his strong suit. He'd certainly proved that, five and a half years ago.

"Sex-crazed idiot," Annie muttered, just as the door swung open and an elderly gentleman shuffled in.

"I *beg* your pardon," he said, while water dripped from his bushy white eyebrows.

Annie's face turned bright pink. "Not you," she said hastily. "I didn't mean... I was talking about..."

Oh, what was the use. She took a deep breath, yanked open the door and plunged out into the deluge.

The train to Stratham was half an hour late, thanks to the weather, and a good thing, too, because it took her twice as long as it should have to get to Penn Station.

She snagged a seat, even though the train was crowded, but her luck ran out after that. The guy who sat down next to her was portly enough to overflow his seat and part of hers, too. And he was in a chatty mood. He started with the weather, went on to the current political scene without stopping for breath. He was coming up fast on the problems of raising teenagers in today's troubled world when Annie made a grab for somebody's discarded newspaper, mumbled "Excuse me," and buried her nose in what turned out to be the business section.

It was rude, perhaps, but she just didn't feel like small talk with a stranger. Her visit with Laurel had upset her, on more than one level. She and Laurel and Susie, Laurel's neighbor, had sat around the kitchen table, drinking coffee and talking, and of the three, only Susie had a husband who'd lived up to his marriage vows.

Annie stared blindly at the newspaper. What was it with men? And with women, for that matter? Didn't they learn? How much grief did it take before you finally figured out that men were just no…

Her breath caught.

Was that a photo of Chase? It certainly was. It was Chase, all right, smiling at the camera and looking pleased with himself and with the world, and why shouldn't he? Standing right beside him, looking gorgeous and as perfect as a paper doll, was Janet Pendleton.

Annie's eyes filled with tears, although she couldn't imagine why. Chase certainly didn't mean anything to her.

"Damn you," she said, in a quavering whisper.

The man beside her stiffened.

"Were you speaking to me, madam?"

She looked up. The guy was looking at her as if she'd just escaped from the asylum.

Annie blinked back her tears.

"You're a man, aren't you?" she said.

Then she crumpled the newspaper, dumped it on the floor, rose from her seat and made her way through the train, to the door.

It was raining in Stratham, too.

Well, why not? The perfect ending to a perfect day, Annie thought grimly, as she made her way through the parking lot to her car. It didn't even pay to run, not when she was wet through and through. What could another soaking possibly matter?

By the time she pulled into her driveway, she was shivering, sniffling, and as close to feeling sorry for herself as she'd ever come. A hot shower and getting into her old terry-cloth robe and a pair of slippers helped. Supper seemed like a good idea, too, but banging open cabinet doors and peering into the fridge didn't spur any creative juices. Finally she gave up, took a diet meal from the freezer and popped it into the microwave.

She was just putting it on the kitchen counter when the doorbell rang.

Annie looked at the clock. It was after seven. Who'd be dropping by at this hour? Unless it was Dawn. A smile lit her face. Dawn and Nick lived only half an hour away and sometimes they dropped in for a quick visit. Everything was fine on that front, thank goodness. Dawn had returned from her honeymoon glowing with happiness, and she'd taken the news that her parents' supposed reconciliation had failed in her stride.

"I'm so sorry, Mom," she'd said, hugging Annie, "but at least you guys tried."

But the visitor at the door wasn't Dawn. It was Deborah Kent, standing in the rain, clutching an enormous box from Angie's Pizza Palace.

"Well?" Deb demanded. "Do I get asked in, or do I have to sit in my car and pig out on all ninety billion calories of an Angie's Deluxe without any help?"

Annie's bleak mood lifted a little. "What kind of friend would I be if I let you suffer such a fate?" she said, taking the box from Deb's hands. "Come on in."

"The kind who ignores repeated phone calls," Deb grumbled as she peeled off her raincoat. "This thing is soaked. You want me to hang it in the laundry room, or what?"

"Just drape it over the back of that chair," Annie said as she headed for the kitchen.

"It'll drip on the floor."

"Trust me, Deb. The floor won't mind. Come and make yourself comfortable while I grab a couple of plates and some napkins."

Deb's eyebrows lifted when she saw the sad little box that had just come out of the microwave oven.

"I see I interrupted an evening of gourmet dining," she said, moving the thing aside with a manicured fingertip.

"Mmm." Annie took two diet Cokes out of the refrigerator and put them on the counter. "You can't imagine what a sacrifice it's going to be to eat a slice of Angie's Deluxe instead."

"A slice?" Deb opened the box, dug out a huge triangle of pizza and deposited it on Annie's plate. "A half of an Angie's Deluxe, is what I'm figuring on." She dug in again and lifted out a piece for herself. "So what's new in your life, anyway?"

"Oh, nothing much." Annie hitched a hip onto a stool. "How've you been?"

"And well you might ask," Deb said indignantly. "For someone's who's supposed to be my best *amiga*, you sure haven't paid much attention to me lately. Don't you ever return phone calls?"

"Of course I do. I've just been busy, that's all. Mmm, this pizza is to die for. And to think I was going to make a meal out of two hundred calories of fat-free, flavor-free yuck. So what if I'll have to give up eating for the rest of the week? This is definitely worth the sacrifice."

"Don't try and pull my leg, Annie Cooper. I can tell a fib from the truth."

"Cross my heart and hope to gain two inches around my hips," Annie said, "this is delicious."

"And can the innocent act." Deb slipped another piece of pizza from the box. "Nobody could be as busy as you claim to be, not unless you've given up eating and sleeping. You've turned into the 'no' girl. No, you don't want to go to the movies, not even when Liam Neeson's on the screen. No, you don't want to go to the mall, even if Lord and Taylor's got a fifty percent clearance."

"I'm sorry, Deb. Really, I am, but as I said, I've been—"

"And," Deb said, stealing a slice of pepperoni from the pizza still in the box, "instead of sharing the good stuff with me, which is the duty of a true-blue friend, you let me find it out all on my own."

Annie's smile stiffened. Nobody knew what had happened on that island. Nobody even knew she'd gone away with Chase, except for Dawn and Nick.

"What 'good stuff'?"

"You know."

"I don't, or I wouldn't be asking. Come on, Deb. What are you talking about?"

Deb shoved aside her plate and pulled the tab on her can of soda.

"Well, for openers, when were you going to tell me you gave Milton Hoffman the old heave-ho?"

"Oh. That."

"Yeah. That. Not that I wasn't happy to hear it. Milton's a nice guy, but he's not for you."

"Where did you hear—"

"I bumped into him at the Stop And Shop the other day." Deb leaned closer. "Did you know that he eats low-fat granola?"

I'm not surprised, Annie said to herself, then scowled for thinking something so unkind.

"Well, so what?" she said staunchly. "That doesn't make him a bad person. Besides, if you wanted to know if I was still seeing him or not, you could have just asked me. You didn't have to buttonhole poor Milton."

"I did not buttonhole poor Milton! He was standing in front of the cereal display, looking unhappy, and I wheeled my cart up to his and said he might want to try the oatmeal, or maybe the All-Bran, depending on his needs. I mean, who knows what's going on under that shiny suit? And he gave me this look that reminded me of a basset hound I once had… Did I know you then? He was the dearest little dog, but—''

"Dammit, Deb, what did Milton say?''

"He just asked if I'd seen you around lately. And I said well, I'd gone to lunch with you a few weeks back. And he said that was more than he'd done. And I said—''

"Whoa.'' Annie held up her hands. "Let me simplify things, okay? Milton's a lovely man. A delightful man. But…''

"But?''

"But, we're just friends.''

"He seemed to think you'd once been something more.'' Deb picked up another piece of pizza. "Like, you'd maybe had serious plans.''

"No! We never…'' Annie put her hands over her face. "Oh gosh. I feel terrible.''

Deb gave a delicate burp. "The pizza's a killer, I admit, but it's not *that* bad.''

"Not the pizza. Milton.''

"You led him on,'' Deb said, clucking her tongue.

"No. Yes. Damn! I suppose I did,'' Annie said, and told Deb about what had happened at the wedding, and how she'd put on an act for Chase's benefit. "But I cleared things up the next week,'' she added quickly. "I explained that—that I'd said some things I hadn't really meant and—and…''

"You broke his little heart,'' Deb said solemnly, and then she grinned and lightly punched Annie in the arm. "Don't look like that! I'm exaggerating. Milton looked absolutely fine. Happier than I've ever seen him, to tell the truth, and halfway through our chat a woman came waltzing over from the produce aisle and looped her arm through his. Her name's Molly Something-or-other, she's new in the English department and it didn't take a genius to figure out what's happening between them when she dropped her head of cabbage into the cart next to his box of granola."

Annie sighed with relief. "I'm glad."

"Milton said to say hi if I saw you, so here I am, saying hi."

"Honestly, Deb—"

"Honestly, Annie, why didn't you tell me you went off and spent the weekend after the wedding with your gorgeous ex?"

Annie turned bright red to the roots of her hair. "What are you talking about?"

"Dawn told me." Deb reached for a piece of pizza, bit into it and chewed thoughtfully. "I met her in the detergent aisle."

"Have you ever considered changing supermarkets?" Annie said sweetly. "What else did my darling daughter tell you?"

"Only that you and Chase went out of town in hopes of a reconciliation, and that it didn't work out. Is that about it?"

"Yes," Annie said. "That's about it."

Deb, who was nobody's fool, eyed her best friend narrowly.

"Maybe your baby girl bought that story," she said, "but I have a few years of observing the human condition on her."

"Meaning?"

"Meaning, you want to tell me what really happened?"

"Nothing happened."

"Annie," Deb said.

The doorbell rang. Annie sent up a silent prayer of thanks.

"Don't think you're off the hook," Deb called as Annie hurried from the kitchen. "I have every intention of picking up the inquisition as soon as you get back." Her voice rose. "You hear?"

Annie rolled her eyes. "I hear," she said, as she flung the door open.

A boy stood on the porch. Rain glittered on his hair and shoulders, and on the yellow panel truck in the driveway.

"Mrs. Annie Cooper?"

Annie looked at the long white box clutched in his arms.

"*Ms.* Annie Cooper," she said. "And I don't want them."

The boy frowned and looked at the tag clipped to the box.

"This is 126 Spruce Street, isn't it?"

"It is, and you're to take those flowers right back where they came from."

"They're roses, ma'am. Long-stemmed, red—"

"I know what they are, and I do not want them." Annie reached behind her and took her pocketbook from the hall table.

"But—"

"Here," she said, handing the boy a ten-dollar bill. "I'm sorry you had to come out in such miserable weather."

"But, ma'am…"

"Good night."

Annie shut the door. She sighed, leaned back against it and closed her eyes.

"What was that about?"

Her eyes flew open. Deb was standing in the hall, staring.

"Nothing. It was a—a mix-up. A delivery of something or other, but the kid had the wrong—"

"I heard the whole thing, Annie. He had the right house and the right woman. He also had a humongous box of roses, and you told him to take them away."

Annie's chin lifted. "I certainly did," she said, marching past Deb into the kitchen. "You want a glass for that Coke, and some ice?"

"I want to know if I'm going crazy. Somebody sends you long-stemmed roses and you don't even want to take a look? You don't even want to ask who they're from?"

Annie took two glasses from the cabinet over the sink and slammed them down on the counter.

"Chase," she said grimly.

"Chase what?"

"Chase sent the roses."

"How do you know? You didn't even—"

"He's been doing it for weeks."

"Your ex has been sending you roses for weeks?"

"Yes. And I've been refusing them." Annie sat down at the counter and picked up her slice of pizza. "Your pizza's going to get cold, if you don't eat it pretty soon."

Deb looked down at her plate, then at Annie.

"Let me get this straight. You went away with your ex, he's been sending you roses ever since, and you really expect me to believe nothing happened between you?"

"That's exactly what I expect you to believe," Annie said, and she burst into tears.

Half an hour later, the pizza had been forgotten, the diet Cokes had been replaced by a bottle of Chianti, Annie's eyes and nose were pink and Deb had heard the whole story.

"The bastard," she said grimly.

"Uh-huh," Annie said, blowing her nose into a paper towel.

"The skunk!"

"That's what he is, all right. Taking me to bed and then telling me how terrific it was—"

"Was it?"

Annie blushed. "Sex was never our problem. Well, not until the very end, when I was so hurt and angry at him for never coming home...."

"Other women, huh?"

"No." Annie blew her nose again. "I mean, not then. At the end, there was somebody, even though Chase said there wasn't."

"Yeah," Deb said, "that's what they always say. So, if it wasn't some foxy broad, why didn't the oaf come home nights?"

"Oh, he came home. Late, that's all. He took all these courses, see, so he could learn the things he needed to build up the business he'd inherited from his father. He worked crazy hours, too. Most days, he'd leave before sunrise and not get back until seven, eight at night."

"Uh-huh."

"And then, when things took off and the company really began to grow, he went to all these parties. Chamber of Commerce things. You know, the sort of stuff you read about in the paper."

"And he left you home. God, the nerve of the man!"

"No. I mean, he took me with him. And then I decided I didn't want to go to these things anymore."

"I can imagine the rest. The jerk went by himself and that's when he began to fool around. He met this society type with a pedigree and a face like an ice sculpture and she was lots more appealing than the house mouse he'd left at home, right?"

"Well—well, no. He didn't meet anybody. Although, eventually, he—he got involved with his secretary."

"How disgustingly trite. His secretary! Will men never learn?"

"He said it wasn't what it seemed to be, but I knew."

"Of course, you knew. Lipstick on his collar, receipts from motels you'd never been to in his pockets, charge account statements for flowers and candy and perfume..."

"No."

"No?"

Annie shook her head. "Well, bills for flowers and candy and perfume, yes. For my birthday, or Christmas, or sometimes just for no reason at all."

"Really," Deb said, arching an eyebrow.

"I'd never have known, except I just—I showed up at his office when he didn't expect me and there she was, wound around him like—like a morning glory vine on a fence post."

"And Chase said he was just taking a speck of dust out of her eye," Deb said, shaking her head.

Annie looked up, her mouth trembling. "Chase said it wasn't what it looked like. His secretary said it, too. She cried and begged me to believe her, she said Chase had never even looked at her cross-eyed but I—"

"But you?"

"But I knew. That he—that she... Because, you know, I'd stopped turning to him in bed, when he reached for me. I couldn't help it." A sob ripped from Annie's throat. "I loved him so much, Deb. So terribly much!"

"Oh, Annie, you poor soul," Deb said, "you still do."

"I don't," Annie said, and she began to weep uncontrollably.

Deb stood up, went to Annie's side and put her arm around her.

"Oh, honey, I never realized. You're crazy about the man."

"No," Annie said in a choked whisper, and then she pulled out of her friend's embrace and threw her arms into the air. "Yes," she said, "and isn't that pathetic? It's true. I *am* crazy about him. I love him with all my heart. I'd even forgive him that fling with his secretary."

"If there was a fling." Annie shot her a look, and Deb shrugged. "Well, it's a possibility, isn't it? I mean, all those stories about bosses and their secretaries…if half of 'em were true, the American economy would grind to a halt. Anyway, why would she have put up such a denial?"

"I don't know. I don't know anything, anymore, only that somewhere along the line, Chase and I lost each other. And I know now that it wasn't all his fault. We were so young when we got married, Deb. I thought marriage was just a fairy tale, you know, the prince rides off with the maiden and they live happily ever after. But it isn't like that. You have to work at a marriage, talk about your goals and your problems."

"And you guys didn't."

Annie shook her head. "No," she said, her voice muffled as she wiped her nose again.

"Well, it's never too late."

"It is." Annie dumped the wet paper towel into the trash and peeled another one off the roll. "It's way too late."

"What about the reconciliation attempt?"

"I told you. It wasn't for real. We just went through the motions, for Dawn."

"But you made love."

"I made love. Chase—Chase just figures we slept together." Annie flashed Deb a fierce look. "And don't you dare tell me it's the same thing."

Deb smiled sadly. "Trust me, Annie. Even I know that it isn't. Well, what happened when the weekend was over? Didn't he suggest seeing each other again?"

"He did." Annie's expression hardened. "He phoned a dozen times. Sure, he wants to see me. For sex. Not for anything else."

"You don't think it would help to see him? Tell him how you feel?"

"No! God, no! It's bad enough I *showed* him how I feel. In bed, I mean. I…" Annie shook her head. "I don't want to talk about it anymore. There's no point. Talking's not going to change—"

The telephone rang. Deb waited for Annie to reach for it.

"Do you want me to take that?" she said, after the phone had rung three times.

Annie shook her head. "Let the machine pick up. I'm not fit to talk to anybody."

The answering machine clicked on.

"*Hi*," Annie's disembodied voice said. "*It's me, but I can't take your call right now. Leave a message and your number, and I'll give you a ring soon as I can.*"

"Very original," Deb said with a smile.

Annie smiled back at her, but her smile disappeared at the sound of Chase's voice.

"Annie? Annie, it's me. Please, babe, pick up if you're there."

"Speak of the devil," Deb whispered.

"Okay," Chase said, and sighed. "But I've got to tell you, it's a problem. How does a guy find out why his ex-wife won't talk to him, if she won't talk to him?"

Annie folded her arms. "He knows why," she hissed to Deb.

"Here's the deal," Chase said, and cleared his throat. "I'm in Puerto Rico. I've got this new client... Hell, Annie, you don't want to hear the whole story. The thing is, I'm flying back to New York tonight. Matter of fact, I'm at the airport down here, right now."

"Fascinating," Annie muttered. "Now he's going to give me his itinerary."

"I'll only be in New York for a couple of days before I head back down to San Juan, and then I'm liable to be gone for a while. And I figured, if there was any last chance you'd see me again..."

"Sleep with him, he means," Annie said, glowering at the telephone.

"I know I've said some of this before, babe, maybe a hundred times to that damn machine of yours, but I guess one last try can't hurt, so here goes. Annie, I know we didn't intend to get involved again. I know we went away together because I dug us into a hole with Dawn. But I thought—I really thought that night we spent together was incredible. And—"

"And we ought to try it again," Annie said coldly. She tried smiling brightly at Deb but it didn't work. Her smile trembled and tears glittered in her eyes.

"And I knew I didn't have any right to ask you to take me back, Annie. That's what I kept thinking, all the way back to Seattle. You've made a new life for yourself, and you've found a new guy, and I could tell you regretted what had happened, the minute you woke up that morning. You were so quiet, with that same shuttered look you had the last few years we were married."

"Annie?" Deb said uncertainly. "Are you hearing this?"

"Annie," Chase said, his voice roughening, "dammit, babe, I love you! If you really want the pansy poet instead of me, you're gonna have to look me in the eye and tell me so. You're gonna have to say, 'Chase, I don't love you anymore. What happened in that cabin was all pretense. I don't want to marry you again and live with you forever...'" Chase drew a ragged breath. "Dammit," he said, "I'm no good at this! You want sensitive, stick with the poet. You want a guy who's never stopped loving you, who'll love you until the day he dies, you don't have to look any further than me."

"Chase," Annie whispered, "oh, Chase..."

"The only lie I told you that entire weekend was when I said I was engaged to Janet Pendleton. Janet's a nice woman. I like her. But I don't love her. I told her that, a few days ago. I could never love anyone, except you."

"Annie," Deb said desperately, "pick up the phone!"

"They're calling my flight, babe, but hell, I'm not getting on! I changed my plans. I'm gonna fly to Boston instead. I'll be at your door in a few hours and I'm warning you, if you don't open it when I ring that bell, so help me, I'll bust it dow—"

Annie made a dive for the phone, but it was too late. All she heard when she picked it up was a dial tone.

"Annie," Deb said, "what are you going to do?"

Annie's smile glittered. "Boston," she said, "here I come."

It was raining in Boston, too.

All flights, departing and arriving, were delayed, the soothing voice over the public address system kept repeating.

The terminal was jammed with weary travelers. Bodies were draped everywhere as people tried to snatch some sleep. There were lines at the ladies' rooms, at the snack counters, at the newsstands. Babies screamed, irate passengers argued with overworked ticket agents and Annie noticed absolutely none of it.

She kept up her vigil at Gate Nine, her eyes glued to the arrivals board, waiting. And waiting.

She wasn't even sure she was waiting in the right place and if she wasn't—if she wasn't, she'd just about run out of options.

It had seemed such a wonderful idea, to go to Boston and meet Chase as he arrived. She'd pictured his face, when he saw her waiting for him; she'd imagined running to him and having his arms close around her.

Halfway to Logan Airport, it had occurred to her that she had no idea what airline Chase was flying.

Her foot had eased off the accelerator. Maybe she should go back.

Back? To pace from one room to another? To go crazy as she waited? No. She couldn't do that. That was why she'd thrown on jeans, sneakers and a T-shirt in the first place, and dashed to her car. She needed to be doing something, or she'd go crazy.

She had to see Chase the minute he stepped off the plane, had to fly into his arms and tell him she had never stopped loving him.

So she'd stepped down, hard, on the pedal again.

By the time she'd reached the airport, she'd had a plan. Well, a plan of sorts.

She'd gone to the first information desk she saw.

"Excuse me," she'd said politely, "but could you tell me what flights are coming in this evening from Puerto Rico?"

"What airline?" the clerk had asked, and Annie had smiled and said, unfortunately, she really didn't know what airline. Was that a problem?

It was, but not an insurmountable one. Annie knew the time Chase's New York-bound flight had boarded. If he'd managed to get himself ticketed on a flight to

Boston instead, it would have to have gone out sometime after that.

That narrowed things down a bit, the clerk said.

There were only three possible flights Chase could have taken. They were on three different airlines, and they came in minutes apart. Annie's plan, therefore, was simple. She'd wait for the first flight and if Chase wasn't one of the deplaning passengers, she'd rush to the next gate and wait again. If necessary, she'd do the same thing a third time.

"Good luck," the clerk had called, as Annie had hurried away.

The plan had seemed logical.

Now, she was beginning to wonder.

Flight one had arrived and disgorged what had looked like a full load of passengers.

Chase had not been among them.

Annie had hurried to the next gate. She'd gotten there out of breath, but with two minutes to spare before the door had opened and the arriving passengers had started streaming into the terminal.

She'd watched faces, standing on tiptoe, keeping her fingers crossed and silently chanting Chase's name like a mantra, but it hadn't helped. The last travelers walked into the terminal but he wasn't among them, either.

Now she was at the final gate, waiting for the third and last plane.

What if Chase wasn't on it?

Annie's hands began to tremble. She thrust them deep into the pockets of her jacket.

Maybe he hadn't been able to change his flight plans. Planes could be sold out. You couldn't just change your plans at the last minute and assume you could get a ticket.

For all she knew, Chase might be landing in New

York at this very minute. He might be phoning her, and reaching her answering machine again. It was late; he'd know she'd be home at this hour of the night.

When she didn't take the call, would he assume she'd gotten his message and wasn't interested?

Annie chewed on her lip.

There was another possibility she hadn't even considered until now. Chase could have hung up the phone and suddenly realized that it would be easier if he flew to Bradley Airport, in Hartford. He might be on his way to her house right now. What if he got there and banged on the door? What if she wasn't there to answer?

Would he think she was out, with Milton Hoffman? Would he think she'd gotten his message and didn't want to see him?

"Oh God," she whispered, "please, please, please…"

God didn't seem to be listening. The last few stragglers had emerged from the ramp that led to the plane.

Chase wasn't one of them.

Tears spilled down Annie's cheeks.

Maybe the simple truth was that he'd changed his mind.

A sob burst from her throat. A couple standing nearby looked at her curiously. She knew how she must look, in her ratty outfit, with her hair all curly and wild from the rain and now with tears coursing down her face, but she didn't care.

Nothing mattered, now that she'd lost Chase a second time.

She turned, jammed her hands into her pockets and started walking.

"Annie?"

What fools they'd been, the two of them. So in love,

and so unable to connect about the things that really mattered.

"Annie?"

There would never be another love in her life. Chase would stay in her heart, forever.

"Annie!"

Hands closed around her shoulders, hands that were familiar and dear.

"Chase?" Annie whispered, and she spun around and saw her husband.

They stared at each other wordlessly, and then Chase opened his arms and gathered her in. She threw her arms around his neck and they clung to each other, oblivious to the people watching and smiling, to the noise and the announcements.

A long minute later, Chase led Annie off into a corner.

"Annie, darling." He took her face between his hands. She was so beautiful. So perfect. His eyes blurred as he bent and brushed his lips against hers. "I'm sorry, sweetheart," he whispered. "I never meant to hurt you. I always loved you, Annie. Everything I did, babe—the long hours, the networking, the meetings—it was all for you. I wanted you to have everything. I wanted you to be proud of me, to be glad you were my wife."

Annie put her hands over his and smiled through her tears.

"I was always proud of you. Don't you know that? I wouldn't care if you dug ditches, just as long as you loved me."

Chase gathered her close and kissed her. "Annie Bennett Cooper," he whispered against her mouth, "will you marry me?"

"Oh, yes," Annie said, "oh, yes, Chase, oh, yes."

"Tonight, babe. We can get right on a plane, fly to the Caribbean and get married on Saint John Island."

"That's a wonderful idea," she said, and kissed him.

Chase looped his arm around her shoulders. "Come on. Let's find the ticket counter."

Halfway to the escalator, he came to a stop.

"Wait here a minute," he said. He brushed a kiss over her mouth, and hurried into one of the shops that dotted the terminal.

Annie looked in the window. A huge vase stood behind the glass, filled with red roses. As she watched, Chase pulled out his wallet and spoke to the clerk. Seconds later, he stood before Annie again, holding one perfect red rose in his hand.

"Do you remember that night, years ago?" he asked. "I'd gotten my first big break, and I brought you one rose..."

Did she remember? Annie's smile trembled. "Yes."

"I love you as much now as I did then, babe." His voice turned husky. "If it's possible, I love you even more."

Annie took the rose from him.

"I'll never stop loving you, Chase," she whispered, and she went into her husband's arms.

EPILOGUE

IT WAS THE DAY AFTER Christmas, and the Cooper clan was gathered in Annie and Chase's living room.

"There's no way your father and I can eat all these leftovers by ourselves," Annie had said, when she'd phoned Dawn and asked if she and Nick would come by for dinner.

"You don't have to convince me, Mom," Dawn had replied, with a smile in her voice. "If there's one thing I still don't love about being a wife, it's cooking."

Now, as Annie sat on the sofa beside her husband, with his arm curled tightly around her shoulders, she looked around her at her family and knew that she had never been happier.

Dawn and Nick were sitting cross-legged beside the big spruce tree Chase had wrestled through the door last week.

"It'll never fit," he'd groaned, as he'd lugged the tree toward the living room.

"Of course it'll fit," Annie had insisted, and it had—after Chase had lopped off two feet with a saw.

Annie's sister, Laurel, was there, too, standing under the sprig of mistletoe Chase had hung in the living room entryway. Annie smiled. Laurel and her gorgeous husband, Damian, were kissing each other as if nobody else existed. As Annie watched, Damian drew back a little, smiled at Laurel and lay his hand gently on her huge belly. He said something that brought a rosy flush to Laurel's cheeks.

Annie smiled and looked away, toward her friend,

Deb, who was sitting before the fireplace, deep in conversation with a man—a very nice man—whom she'd met a couple of months ago.

"In the supermarket?" Annie had asked teasingly.

Deb had blushed. "In the library, but if you tell that to anybody, I'll deny everything."

Annie sighed and put her head on Chase's shoulder. What a difference a few months could make. She'd been so unhappy this past summer, and now—and now, her heart was almost unbearably filled with joy.

"Babe?"

She looked up. Chase smiled at her.

"You think it's time to tell them our plans?"

Annie smiled back at her husband. They'd been married for months now, and every day still felt like part of their honeymoon.

"Yes," she said. "Let's."

Chase grinned and kissed her. Then, holding her hand and drawing her up with him, he rose to his feet.

"Okay, everybody," he said, "listen up."

Everyone turned and looked at Chase and Annie. Chase cleared his throat.

"Annie and I had a problem..."

Long, deep groans echoed around the room.

Chase laughed and drew Annie closer.

"The problem was, where were we going to live? Annie had this old house that she loved. And I had a condo that I was pretty happy with, in New York."

"Don't tell us," Deb said. "You guys have decided to pitch a tent on a beach, in Tahiti."

Chase and Annie laughed along with everybody else, and then Chase held up his hand.

"And then, there was Annie's flower business and my construction company. As I say, we had a problem." He looked down at his wife and smiled. "Tell 'em how we solved it, babe."

"Well," Annie said, "when we thought about it, it was really a cinch."

"I told you," Deb said. "The tent, on the beach in Tahiti."

"We bought an island," Annie said, "off the Washington coast."

Dawn scrambled to her feet. "*An* island, Mom? Or *your* island?"

Annie blushed. "Our island. Your father spoke to Mr. Tanaka and convinced him that there was another island for sale up the coast that would be much more to his liking."

"I'm going to build us a house," Chase said.

"Isn't there a house there already?"

Chase and Annie smiled at each other. "Yes," Annie said softly, "a very handsome one...but we've decided we want something of our own. Something—something cozier." She looked at the people gathered around them. "Chase will build our house, and I'm going to put in a garden, and after that, we're going to combine forces. Cooper and Cooper, Landscape and House Design." She grinned. "Please notice that I get top billing."

Everyone laughed, and then Dawn clapped her hands.

"Well," she said, "as long as it's announcement time, I have one of my own." She smiled happily. "I'm going back to school. I signed up for the spring semester."

Annie let out a shriek. "Oh, baby, that's wonderful news!"

Nick smiled proudly and put his arm around his wife's waist. "It is, isn't it? Dawn will have her degree four years from now, and then—" A blush stole over his handsome features. "And then," he said, ducking his head, "we're going to start a family."

"Way to go, Nick," Damian called out. He winked at his wife, who stood smiling in the circle of his arms. "Of course, by then Laurel and I will probably be working on baby number two, or maybe three."

Everyone whistled and cheered.

"All right," Deb said briskly, "that's enough of this nonsense. You guys don't have a monopoly on good news, you know." She took a deep breath, looked up at the smiling man at her side and looped her arm through his. "Arthur and I have decided to tie the knot. And before anybody says we're tying it around each other's throats, let me make it perfectly clear that what I mean is, he's asked me to marry him." Deb's voice softened. "And I said I would so—it's too late to back out, Arthur, because now I've got witnesses."

In the laughter and good-natured banter that followed, it was simple for Annie and Chase to drift off into the kitchen, alone.

Chase took Annie in his arms.

"You know," he said, "after all these happy announcements, I've been thinking…"

She smiled up at him. "Yes?"

"Well," he said, "well…"

"Well, what?"

Chase smiled back at her. "Maybe we ought to reconsider those plans for the new house. I mean, heck, right down the hall from where our bedroom's going to be—wouldn't that be a great place to put a nursery?"

Annie looked deep into the eyes of her husband. Then she smiled, looped her arms around his neck, brought his head down to hers and kissed him.